IF YOU CROSS

THE RIVER

IF YOU CROSS

THE RIVER

A Novel

GENEVIÈVE DAMAS

Translated from the French by

JODY GLADDING

MILKWEED EDITIONS

First published in French. Original edition: "Si tu passes la rivière," © 2011 Éditions Luce Wilquin, Avin, Belgium
© 2019, English translation by Jody Gladding

Published 2019 by Milkweed Editions
Printed in the United States of America
Cover design by Mary Austin Speaker
Cover artwork by Jim Musil
Author photos by Craig Line (Gladding) and Cici Olsson (Damas)
19 20 21 22 23   5 4 3 2 1
First Edition

Milkweed Editions, an independent nonprofit publisher, gratefully acknowledges sustaining support from the Ballard Spahr Foundation; the Jerome Foundation; the McKnight Foundation; the National Endowment for the Arts; the Target Foundation; and other generous contributions from foundations, corporations, and individuals. Also, this activity is made possible by the voters of Minnesota through a Minnesota State Arts Board Operating Support grant, thanks to a legislative appropriation from the arts and cultural heritage fund, and a grant from Wells Fargo. For a full listing of Milkweed Editions supporters, please visit milkweed.org.

Library of Congress Cataloging-in-Publication Data

Names: Damas, Geneviève, author. | Gladding, Jody, 1955- translator.
Title: If you cross the river : a novel / Geneviève Damas ; translated from the French by Jody Gladding.
Other titles: Si tu passes la riviére. English
Description: Minneapolis : Milkweed Editions, 2019.
Identifiers: LCCN 2017036825 (print) | LCCN 2017038472 (ebook) | ISBN 9781571319357 (ebook) | ISBN 9781571311207 (pbk. : alk. paper)
Classification: LCC PQ2704.A443 (ebook) | LCC PQ2704.A443 S513 2019 (print) |
DDC 843/.92--dc23
LC record available at https://lccn.loc.gov/2017036825

To Baptiste, my wolf of wolves.

And to those who have lost everything except honor.

IF YOU CROSS

THE RIVER

"If you cross the river, if you cross the river," said the father, "you'll never set foot in this house again. If you go to the other side, you better watch out, if you go to the other side." I was small then when he said that to me for the first time. I came halfway to his shoulder, just barely, and I cheated a little by standing on tiptoes to be taller, cheated to be closer to my brothers who were a good head taller than the father when he was doubled over his pitchfork. I was small then, but I remember it. He was looking straight ahead, as if the hill and the forest in the distance didn't exist, as if the remains of the burned buildings were there just for the crows, as if nothing mattered anymore, nothing, and his gaze went right through everything.

"Stop bawling at me like a cow," is what I said to him, "stop bawling. I don't want anything to do with the other side. Ever. You don't have to go and get yourself all worked up. Your François, he's staying here. That won't ever change."

I wasn't lying when I said that, I meant it. Then my father scratched the top of my head and back as if he were calming down. Then he went back to getting in the hay because that was one heck of a job for us, and you had to think of the animals who worked as hard as you did, if not harder, who made you a gift of their hides, even their bones.

I was never afraid of work. Even though I was the smallest, I did my share like anyone else, like the older ones, and that was another reason why the father wanted to keep me near him for sure, to keep me from running off to the other side of the river where life led you and you never came back the same.

-»-<-

None of us had ever taken off for the other side. Except Maryse, but that, that was a long time ago and the father, for days on end he had howled about it so that no one ever mentioned it again, as if she'd never existed, Maryse, for fear of a beating that would leave you black-and-blue for weeks. But me, in my head, I was nowhere near forgetting that we'd had a Maryse, that she was gentle and fair and that sometimes she stroked my head and called me Fifi. Even the crown of my skull remembered, even my hair that struggled against the comb when she helped me get dressed on Sundays for our walk on the main road, even my teeth when they smiled. There were times at night when they were all in bed, my brothers, and the father, he was busy with his own affairs, when I sometimes pushed open the door to Maryse's room, which hadn't changed, where no one went anymore, where I could see that the table, the chair, and the bed had been waiting all this time for her to come back one day, for her to enter, light the small lamp, for her to untie her boots (she wouldn't put them under the bed carefully as usual), for her to leave them lying there, her boots, for her to throw her coat over the chair, for her to drop her bag, and then for her to lie down on her bed still fully dressed, and for her to sing her song. So, like Maryse's things, I waited, I took up my broom and dustcloth to wipe away the time that passed and the dust like fallen snow on everything Maryse had known, so that when my sister returned, everything would be ready, everything would be intact, just as before, and the bad days when the father no longer laughed and only bawled at the world would be nothing more than nightmares that ended with the morning light.

I didn't really know why Maryse had up and fled like that one day. I didn't really know. I was watching the pigs that morning. I was watching them because no one else wanted to and because I was the smallest. And also all that dirt, that never mattered to me, I was at home in the dust and the wind. It was warm and everything was peaceful along the paths I saw around me, the river running straight ahead and the fish living their fishy lives. And then I heard the father bawling in the courtyard, bawling like a madman, and strange sounds that I didn't understand because I'd never heard anyone cry. In our house, no one cried, inside there were tears, but outside it was dry. So I couldn't know before I saw her coming, tears streaming down her face and a big bag on her back. She was red, my sister, who was usually so pale, and she marched along without seeing me.

"Maryse," I said, "Maryse," and I could hear the father in the courtyard still bawling and the voice of the priest and, from time to time, one of my brothers trying to get a word in edgewise, but without any effect it seemed. And Maryse kept walking straight ahead, toward the river, and me, I ran after her, but I had no words to hold her back, nothing but "Maryse, Maryse," and the roaring of the river got closer and we were right at the edge of the water, and at that moment I was thinking that after days in the fields, in the evening when I came home tired and dirty, the face that I sought out, the face that I waited for, it was Maryse's face, the light in her eyes and especially when she said, "How were the pigs today, Fifi?" because she was the only one who asked, because no one said anything to me except to tell me there was something to do, what pigs had to be killed, and otherwise it was like talking to the wind. I couldn't imagine life without the light in Maryse's eyes, that's why I said "Maryse, Maryse," even though I saw it coming and it seemed to me that now the river was throwing water in my face. Maryse took off her boots, she hitched up her skirt, she looked at me and said, "I won't ever come back, ever, this is it." Then I clung to her waist like a tick to a pig's back and I whispered, "Maryse, Maryse." She gently unwrapped my arms, I was small and weak then, she stroked my hair, "My Fifi," she said and she didn't mind even though I smelled of mud and animal dung, "My Fifi." She took one step into the river, then another, and I had all the words in my head to call her back, to beg her to take me with her, me, I didn't even know how to swim, but no, nothing, I stood there, small and stupid, watching my sister in the water, getting farther away with each step and all I could say was "Maryse, Maryse," because maybe it's like that when life takes away from you the most beautiful thing it gave you, there's nothing to say but let the rivers flow. I watched her for a long time, my sister, becoming small and then disappearing on the other side of the water where we never went, where we were forbidden to go, until I felt a blow on my skull and I understood by the father's look that it was time for supper.

→>-<←

I went on spending my days with the pigs. A pig seems stupid and dirty and without grace if you don't look carefully. That's because of the mud. But the mud is nothing, it doesn't have anything to do with the pig. If you really look at the pig, if you really look at it, its eyes are the first thing you see. Its eyes aren't stupid or dirty or without grace, just small, soft, and fragile. If you really look into the eyes of a pig, you can see its soul. A pig must have a soul, everyone has one, even you, even me, even the ants, even the leaves. That's why they shouldn't be killed for nothing. If you kill a pig, you must eat all of it, so that its soul comes to find your own and gives you the strength to go on your way. Me, if I can stand up straight, that's because I have all the pigs inside me. And you too and everyone. Sometimes the pigs keep me warm. What comforts me when I'm crying inside is that all the pigs I've eaten, they're with me, crying inside.

With pigs, what's beautiful is birth. Even if it's frightening, because you never know what's going to happen with birth. The sow is afraid too, you can see it in her eyes and, at that moment, you tell yourself that you're alike, you and her. And if you're alike, you aren't truly alone anymore. Pigs are very beautiful when they're born, pink and soft. Like puppies but prettier because you know they won't bite. Me, I always think that if I had to roam the world and go to the other side of the river (which will never happen for sure, like I hissed at the father), I wouldn't take a donkey or a cow with me, I'd take a pig, a newborn pig. And when it couldn't go on, my pig, across the mountains, the valleys, and maybe even the seas, I would take it in my arms and I would put it over my shoulders like the priest's shepherd who rescued the lost sheep from the precipice.

→>◄─

Roger the priest. We never went into his house with a cross. The father said that just thinking of stepping foot in there got him down. Me, I didn't know. I saw him, Roger, riding his bicycle every day along the path beside the field, and he raised his biretta to me and called out, "How's it going, François?" And me, I waved because it was no use answering, he wouldn't have heard me, he was already well past on his bike. In his bag he always carried books, a white cloth with a cross, and bread to give to those who needed it. That shoulder bag of Roger's worried me, because I put it in the same category as Maryse's sack, and I wanted to know, me who had promised the father never to leave home, I wanted to know what you took with you when you went away. So one morning I stood there in the middle of the path to wait for him, him, with his cassock hitched up around his knees so it wouldn't get caught in the spokes of his bicycle, and I said, "Hello, Curé, empty your bag," and I saw in his eyes that he was afraid I would take it from him, his bag, just like that, because I was younger and stronger, because it makes a man big and strong when he spends all his days breathing the meadow air and watching the pigs. So Roger, he showed me. The cloth with the cross I couldn't care less about, like stones in the path, the bread was completely flat, but the books, the books I wanted to touch to see if they were soft, as soft as my pigs when I took them in my arms. They were different, colder, but inside one of them were pictures like I'd never seen before, drawings with gold and figures in faraway countries. The curé noticed that the book set something going in my brain, the book and the pictures he called holy, and even though he was frightened, he saw I wasn't a bad sort. So he asked me if I'd like it, his book, if I'd like it for myself. "Yes," I said, "yes," and I took it from him and hurried back to my field, because I saw the father below in the courtyard waving his arms and I knew that he shouldn't see him, this Roger in his cassock, especially since Maryse left, and I told myself that, all in all, it would be better to leave now that I had the answer to my question. The book I slid into my pants, and that first day I didn't dare take it out. I stayed straight as a board, walking with my legs apart, even though that evening the father asked me if I'd peed my pants like a peasant and he and my brothers laughed. But eventually, when no one was around, under the oak tree, I opened the book and I looked at it so long I almost wore it out. In it there was a woman with blond hair who held a child in her arms, on each page the child grew, but the woman always stayed the same, young and beautiful, and smiling. In the evening I hid the book under Maryse's mattress so that my brothers wouldn't take it from me, because at our house everything belonged to everyone and nothing just to me.

Sometimes I told myself stories with the book's pictures. They always began the same way. There was a child who was lost among the farm animals. But the blond woman, who was like a fairy, took him in her arms and carried him to the ends of the earth, where they came to the sea. There these two had lots of adventures, and the blond woman was always smiling, she made the child a picnic lunch and a bed, she knitted him a sweater, she danced with him. Sometimes she told him stories. Sometimes they swam with the dolphins. Sometimes they gazed at the stars. At first, it did me good to dream of the blond woman and all the things she might do with the lost child, but little by little, it began to mess with my head and everything below it. I thought about her so much that I seemed to see her behind every tree and every blade of grass. I dreamed that she took me too, took me where I'd promised never to go because except for Maryse, all my life is here. So then I wasn't looking at the pigs anymore, I was seeing them as you see them when you think to yourself they're stupid, they're dirty, they smell bad. I hardly took care of the pigs, I just ran around feeding, slitting throats when I had to, sorting things out. Big old Médard I left for a whole night squealing and bawling on the other side of the pond. At meals, I didn't say anything, just ate my soup because it does you good even when you've just hung around all day outside. My brothers laughed at me, "What'd you see a fly or something, François?" And I got so angry I turned red, because it wasn't a fly, it was something much more beautiful than a fly, the blond woman, there, then gone. I squealed, I bawled, my father gave me a hard smack on the head, and I shut up. At night I lay in bed awake, my blood stirring, tossing and turning, and there was nothing I could do about it. I was sorry I'd ever come across the blond woman in the book who'd taken over my brain and left me no peace.

So I waited for him, Roger the priest, one winter morning in the dark when no one sees you, just to keep the father from yelling, the father who cursed any sort in a cassock. I was hiding in the bushes and the moment I saw him coming with his bicycle light, I shouted, "Hey! Stop!" He was scared as the devil, so he threw himself into the thicket and I had to dash after him like a grass snake on the path in summer threading its way between twigs. But I was quicker, thanks to my experience with pigs, when you have to chase them because they've gotten an idea into their heads that seizes them from ears to tail. I caught him by the feet and pulled hard. He was so frightened, he cried, "Mercy, mercy," wriggling like a sausage that doesn't want to be fried, and I said to him, "It's François, Curé, stop acting like a worm." Then he calmed down, and that was really a good thing because, in less time than it takes to say it, that little tussle had left us both covered with dirt from head to toe.

"What do you want, François?"

So I slipped the book from my pants, the sun was coming up, and I said, "I want to know what she wants."

"Who?"

"The blond woman who takes the lost child from the farm."

"What blond woman?"

He really didn't understand at all, the curé, and maybe it was because of the blow he'd given himself when I'd had him by the feet, because his whole forehead was red and bloody and that wasn't so nice to see. So I opened it, his book, the book that he'd given me, and I showed him the woman I meant.

"Oh! Marie. Marie, the mother of Jesus."

"What does she want from me, Curé?"

"What do you mean, what does she want from you?"

"I see her everywhere, all the time, in my head."

Roger looked at me, then at the book, he smiled, pulled a handkerchief from his pocket, and wiped his forehead. The handkerchief turned red. I repeated it, "What does she want from me? What does she want from me?"

"She talks to you?"

"No, I only see her doing things with the lost child. What does she want from me?"

"They're waiting for me over there. Old Mahieu hasn't much time left. Come see me this evening, at the presbytery. I'll explain what she wants. Alright?"

"Alright."

And he got back on his bike and rode away faster than a stone tumbling down a cliff. Old Mahieu, today was his big day for sure, and Saturday they would lower him into the ground.

The day sped by like a fly's fart and that evening after supper I tried not to get caught daydreaming, get stared at by
my brothers, and then start yelling at my family. I said I was
going out to check on big old Médard who was always getting into trouble, and I took off down the main road, carry-
ing my boots so that no one would hear them echoing when
the wind shifted toward our house. The book, very warm,
was still in my pants. I was a little afraid. This was the first
time I'd set foot in his house. On the way, I thought of everything the father said about curés, priestlings, priests, and
clerics. When Jean-Paul fell off the roof, we didn't even go
in. We went with the casket to the main door and we waited
outside for the curé to bring it to us after he did what he had
to do, and then we lowered it into the ground. I remember
as if it were yesterday. While the curé went about his business, we stood there silently with the father looking at the
clouds, because it did something to us even if he made us
stand there like that, Jean-Paul. It was only Maryse who
cried and every once in a while said, "Curse you," with her
eyes to the ground, and I didn't know if she meant the father, or Jean-Paul, or the lot of us who hadn't had the guts

to do anything. After that, every once in a while, Maryse had taken the path to the presbytery, in the evening, her boots under her arm, until that horrible morning came when she crossed the river.

He was waiting for me, Roger, he had even put out a bowl of his soup for me, but I didn't want it, I had already lapped up my own, and I didn't want to get a fat belly like our Médard or the father since Maryse had gone to the other side. He asked me plenty of questions to get an idea of what was going on in my head. Sometimes there were miracles, he said, and then his Marie might really want something from me. But after a few minutes, he decided this was no miracle, not worth a bean. He kept using words like "original," "particular," "special." All to say that I was strange and came from an even stranger family and that the village wondered about us. After what seemed like forever, I'd had enough, but Roger kept rambling on. I pulled the book from my pants and I said, "That's enough, Curé, that's enough." Then he took the book and stopped for a moment, maybe because of the smell that called up the farm, the pigs, and all the time I'd spent looking them straight in the eye, and he held the book out before me and leafed through the pages. I pointed at each picture, and Roger, he told the story of the blond woman. It was a story full of happiness and suffering, and misfortune as well. I was glad to know her better, this blond woman, at the same time as it did something to me because I felt that by knowing everything, I couldn't dream about her ever again, and when he saw me all quiet and melancholy, I think that Roger really felt sorry. He said something like, "Don't be sad, François." I jumped up because I don't like it when anyone calls me sad. I can be sad like everyone else, but I don't show it. With the father, if I'm sad, I could get smacked or be called a woman, and get laughed at, like they laughed at Jean-Paul. That's why I'm never sad, except when I go into Maryse's room, and that's only late at night when they're fast asleep. That's why I jumped to my feet.

But Roger had lots of tricks up his sleeve. He said, "What would you say, François, if I told you other stories, tell me, would you like that?" I answered, "I'd have to see, I'm not Maryse," I said, "not Maryse at all, because it could well be that you put it into her head to cross the river, why not, just start swimming, just hearing those fine stories that soften the heart and make you think someone's sad when they aren't sad at all." Roger seemed upset, he frowned and then he said, "That's not why Maryse came to see me, that's not why." There was a long silence while Roger stared straight into my eyes. I had nothing more to do in his house now but shift my weight from one leg to the other, then all of a sudden I sprang up and slipped through the open window to go back home. Afterwards I cursed myself for having left so quickly because the book, I'd forgotten it on the table, but luckily it remained so stamped in my head that I really thought I would never need to leaf through it again.

➤➤⟵⟵

My brothers, I still haven't talked about them. Up until now, I've just said "brothers," as if they formed one whole, so how would you know that there are two of them, as different to look at as grains of wheat and rye? First, there's Jules. Jules, the second of us, who's a head taller than us and who took Maryse's place at the table. Jules has a strong voice and the shoulders to go with it. When he calls your name and looks at you, you right away duck to avoid blows, because Jules, you'd guess right off that he was his father's son. He resembles him as one ham looks just like another. But over the course of time, I learned that with Jules, if you slip away quietly, if you make like you're hardworking and obedient, you can dance the jig behind his back, because Jules knows only what he sees. What might be smoldering under the embers he can't imagine.

Jules, his job is to take care of the machines. Machines

he knows. "It's the role that falls to the oldest," he says. That's what Jules has always said, for as long as I can remember. But he isn't the oldest. Not at all, not one bit. The oldest of us is Maryse. That's what I repeated to myself at night in bed when Jules clouted me for having hidden Oscar because I didn't want anyone to eat him, the one who was my friend. He was always with me, Oscar, he stuck close beside me. Sometimes I told myself that here was a dog in a pig's body. When Jules burst out one evening, "It's Oscar's turn," my legs started trembling, so I made a hole in the fence and I led him through to the other side, to the edge of the river, and I said I'd lost him, that filthy pig! And in the evening I brought him peelings, told him about my day, and so on. Two weeks that lasted, and then one afternoon I heard cries, the cries of a pig being bled, and the blood began to throb in my head. I ran into the courtyard and saw it was Oscar, my Oscar. I arrived just soon enough to see the light in his eyes one last time. He looked at me. And me, I looked at him and I wanted to tell him that I had never wanted this, that if I could have, I would have helped him cross the river, but I could only repeat, "Oscar, Oscar," holding him closer with his blood running down my neck, because I'm an idiot who can't say anything, who can't stop anything because I don't have the words, and if I had the words I would protect him, I would have protected him, my Oscar, though no words were needed for us to love each other. For the moment, Jules did nothing, but in the evening when I refused to eat, he beat me because I had disobeyed and because "you can never do that to the oldest," he said. "Look at me, François, I'm going to beat you until you get that into your head." I clenched my jaw so as not to cry out, not to swallow my pig. It wasn't that I didn't want to have Oscar in my belly, it was just that I didn't deserve him. You don't deserve the friend you can't defend. It isn't fair to ask him to go with you on your way. So I took Oscar's teeth and I made them into a necklace. And I thought to myself, it's Maryse who's the oldest of us. Until she took off.

But I also have to say that a few months later, Jules came back from town with the accordion. And that was no small thing. It was on a Tuesday, he came back from looking after the tractors, and he brought this thing with mother-of-pearl buttons. Immediately I recognized it. At village festivals, there's always one like it that makes us dance, lifting our feet and waving our arms. Forgetting that we're part of the earth, with our feet on the ground, and that we'll never become birds. When he saw me looking at it, Jules said to me, "You can take it if you want." He had to repeat it three times because Jules and me, we rarely talked and, since Oscar, we could never talk to each other at all anymore. But I wanted the accordion, I really wanted it. I placed my fingers over it, I took it into the meadow, and it sang its song to me. Its song of loneliness and freedom, Maryse's song too, since I hadn't forgotten it, and Oscar's song that I sang in my head so as not to lose it, ever. That was one hell of a day, that one.

The second brother, that's Arthur, he's blond with straight hair, while Jules is dark as a forest in the middle of winter. Arthur is the fourth of us since Jean-Paul was the third. But that's another story that shouldn't be stirred up from the bottom, like a pot of soup left to cook too long. Arthur, he's handsome as an ox, with blue eyes you could fall into if you knew how to swim. At market, the girls keep an eye on him, spying on him right behind our stall. He pretends not to notice, so much so that they do it more and more, going back and forth in front of the hams, laughing and hiding behind the cowshed where he hitches up their skirts and they let out their stupid cries, like my pigs sometimes. Arthur, he has his fits of rage some days, so it's better not to cross his path. You can see it right away, beer gets to him and he gets the evil eye. Then he starts throwing anything he can find in your direction, and too bad for you if it's a bike wheel or old Médard or the pitchfork leaning against the wall. You'd be wise to scram. But when he's calm he can be tender as a cow's muzzle, he pats you on the shoulder and says to you, "That's good, François." Sometimes too you see his eye wander, his face twist, and he's lost to us. He falls on the ground and you have to hold his tongue so he doesn't swallow it, otherwise he's done for.

Arthur's job is the market. Everything our hands, arms, and legs make on the farm my brother takes to make money from them. He's the one who goes out, he's the one who knows the paths, the small roads, the big roads, and the ones that are even bigger still. Sometimes I got to go with him, after Jean-Paul fell from the roof and he was crying all the time, Arthur, beating his breast and wailing, "It's my fault." I don't even know why I went those days, because nothing sold, nothing at all. You'd think that our cheeses, our ham, and our sausage weren't worth a thing anymore since our third one had thrown himself from the roof. Still I held his hand, Arthur's, when he drove the truck, to take away his pain and mine with it, I held his hand, looking at the countryside with the sun rising and the sun setting as it left for the other side of the world. And in that moment, I saw fields and fields as far as the eye could see, vaster than ours, vaster than mine where my pigs grazed.

+>-<+

However much they were different, my two brothers, when it came to some things, they understood each other like the moon and the stars. Things like money, like, "We'll never set foot in your church, Curé," like, "The less you talk, the better, if you have something to say, keep quiet, if you're happy, keep quiet, if you're unhappy, keep quiet. Keep quiet, keep quiet, keep quiet." That might have had something to do with the mother.

+>-<+

A mother, I imagine that I must have had one. The pigs all have one, why not me? However much I search my brain, I can't see her, only the face of Maryse, who held my hand and stroked my forehead saying, "Fifi," when I had the chicken pox. No photos of our mother, just the blow when I asked the father about her, and his eyes looking off into nowhere, and the big silence that followed.

That got me to worrying in my head. One afternoon when the father had gone for his nap behind the vegetable garden, I left my pigs, and just like a man I marched right up into his room. I must have gotten my courage from the trace of that mother I must have had, who must have carried me in her arms with love and kindness like the blond woman on the farm. All that was pounding in my skull before I opened the door, because no one ever went into the father's room. Not ever. Who knows why. There wasn't anything in that room except the bed, which wasn't even made up, as if no one lived there. It was no nicer than mine, this room, only bigger, with an open window looking out to the main road. The walls were bare, painted a color that had once been white, and in places there were whiter patches as if frames or photos had hung there or other things that someone had suddenly decided to take down. You could still see the nails in some places. I looked into the big armoire that creaked when you opened it: pants, suspenders, work boots, shorts, shirts, sweaters with the strong odor of the father rising from them. Under the bed, boxes covered with dust. I took one of them out to look. It held pictures of our place: the farm, the pig field, the wheat and rye fields, the narrow path, the riverbank. It looked just like now except for lots more flowers, since now, the father didn't want any flowers, they made him bristle so that every hair on his body stood on end. Flowers big and small, in trays and pots, but also wild along paths, hanging in clusters, and growing in beds. Looking carefully, I also saw that the river wasn't the same in these pictures as now. It had a bridge, a wooden bridge, and behind it you could see distinctly, if you looked, a farm. A farmhouse and then a barn and also a cowshed, whereas now, on the other side of the river, you can't see anything at all except for some old burned collapsing walls without any roofs over them and, if it weren't for Maryse, frankly, I'd have no interest in going there just to get my legs and whole body all scratched by thorns and nettles.

As I was reaching for the other box, I heard the father's footsteps and I threw myself under the bed so he wouldn't catch me and beat the holy crap out of me, my head, neck, my whole back, and everything below it. I felt him sit down on the mattress, which crushed my shoulders and smashed my nose into the boxes and the dust. I had to keep myself from sneezing. I saw the father slide his toes out of his work boots, his fingers rubbing between each of them as he sighed, then I saw his feet go into his Sunday shoes and leave again as they had come. I held my breath, and when everything fell silent, in a flash, I escaped through the window and went back to my pigs, my heart pounding at the thought of getting caught.

→→←←

Since Oscar's death, I'd found another one to talk to. If with Oscar it was love at first sight, with this one, I must admit, I gave some thought to my choice. With my old pig I had seen immediately that we were alike: his way of looking, of examining; the air he adopted before he did something, no hurry, no rage, and then bam! off I went; his gentleness; his way of staying clean despite the mud. But I ought to have known, the males always end up in the sausage line. Whereas the females, they give you piglets, so you think twice before slapping them on your bread. So, I had to choose one of them. That would do me ever so much good since Maryse had taken off. As I figured it, there were only three possibilities: Dora, Daisy, and Hyménée. I had eliminated the others, all twenty-two of them, as either too old or too young. I needed one who had experience, or else what can you tell her if she doesn't understand anything? But if she were too old, she would give me that knowing look, like my brothers or father, who thought they knew everything already every time I opened my mouth.

Dora was sweet, almost cuddly. The problem was she liked to spend her time with big old Médard, to follow him everywhere, even into holes he couldn't get out of anymore. That seemed odd to me, and I thought to myself, it's true she's bold but she's also stupid and scatterbrained like those sows who get themselves into terrible situations they can't get out of. So is that what would happen with us, her grunting and me forever pulling her out of the rotten holes she got herself into, chasing someone else? And who would I rely on? That would never work.

Daisy was more boorish, but wily. Who could unearth mushrooms on the first try? Who eluded the grass snake without wearing herself out? Who found the shortest way back to the farm? Daisy. At the same time, I found her quite ugly. Roger, he says that love forgives all, even ugliness, and he may be right, but at the same time I don't see why he opens his trap because he doesn't know a thing about love, always upright as a candle in his cassock that he hitches up only to piss against a wall or ride a bike. Daisy was ugly. Quite ugly. A little bloated, low to the ground, with a ripped ear that our old dog had bitten off after a fit of convulsions. She was three colors: light, medium, and dark. However much I considered it from different angles, she didn't appeal to me. I felt something like pity for her. I would always have to be careful to control myself when we argued because sometimes when you love someone you'll just say anything when you're angry, you'll yell and blurt out insults, just to get back at the other one who's trampling your heart. But in this case, my insults would have seemed true.

And I wouldn't have been able to look Daisy in her gentle eyes anymore.

That left only Hyménée. It was a funny name, Hyménée, for an almost two-year-old sow. But it had come from Maryse, who had talked about a little sow she had named Hyménée after a book someone had read to her—our mother?—or she had read, I don't know, when she was six or seven, because all five of us had taken our turn with the pigs. But Hyménée had lived for only ten days and had died in the arms of Maryse, who had cried when the little pink ball turned gray. So when I saw Renate's eight piglets, long after Maryse left, I didn't name the females right away. I waited because death always comes to claim its share, that's the rule, even for us. I waited for the new moon and then through each of the quarter moons until it was completely full. And by then there was only one left who would one day become a sow. And I named her Hyménée without knowing, to tell the truth, if that would bring good luck or not, Hyménée, just like that, for Maryse's return, because me, I believe that someday Maryse will come back—without thinking about it, just like that, one fine morning—even if, by the expression on the priest Roger's face when I said her name, I understood that he didn't believe it at all anymore, that she would come back, who knows why. That one who prays to the Lord, wears the cassock, rides the paths on his bike, and doesn't believe in anything.

Hyménée. She was the one I chose. I rested my hand on her side and I gave her a bit of lettuce that I'd brought in my bag as a token of friendship. I saw the look in her eyes asking if this was not just sweet talk, like when our Arthur picked up girls with his gaze. So I kept my hand there a long time, almost all day and again later, until it was too dark to tell the meadow saffron from the thistle anymore. I hardly looked at the other pigs. And when I threw myself into bed afterward, I felt tired and light. It was no big thing, Hyménée and me, but it was true that we were linked, the two of us. Because what can bring you more joy than being linked to someone, that's what I said to myself. No matter who it is. For me it was Hyménée, but it could have been the robin I saw every morning on the fence or our old dachshund, Sammy, or my father, or whoever you please. The important thing is to be linked with someone who is linked to you. That's why I tell myself, Roger, he may know lots of things, but he's all by himself like the pitchfork leaning against the wall, like the wind in the closet under the stairs, and that's why, with all the due respect and with all his knowledge that scares me, never would I want to be like

him, even if he lives in his big house and almost everyone says hello to him.

→>−<−

Roger. He kept running around in my head, that one, with
what he'd said the last time, that he could tell me other
ones, other stories, as many as I pleased. We told each other
stories, Hyménée and me, you don't need anyone else to
tell each other about the little things: weather, wind in the
branches, how water runs faster some days, pebbles on the
path. But really thinking about it, our stories were always
the same, so much so that one day I thought to myself it
might be good for the two of us to know other ones, so
we could share them by recalling them together, changing
them, and making them into lies, both of us. Maybe too, I
knew that with Roger, I could talk about Maryse someday
without getting a thrashing or simply without fear in my
belly, and also about Jean-Paul, what had happened to Jean-
Paul that day and if it was true that we were all damned for
not doing anything at the time although everyone said it
was clear as day what happened, and finally about a mother,
about my mother, because you had to have a mother since
everyone has one—like I said already—even big old

Médard, even our dachshund, Sammy, even Hyménée since she had Renate.

So one evening, boots in hand, I just went to his house, without telling anyone, just Hyménée, and I tapped on his shutter. It took him some time to react, so I tapped hard, harder, and then knocked. Finally I heard his voice, as though asleep: "What's all this racket?" "It's me, Roger," I said, "it's me." I heard him talking to someone else, and his voice sounded relieved, "It's nothing. It's François from the last farm, don't worry." And he stuck his head out the window. It was the first time I'd seen him without his cassock, he was naked from the waist up, and, well, without his cassock, Roger didn't look like Roger.

"What is it, François?"

"The stories, Curé, I'm here for the stories. Can I come in?"

He seemed annoyed. "Not tonight, I'm busy."

"I can wait if you want, Roger, I've got plenty of time, do what you have to do."

He said again, "Not tonight, tomorrow if you want."

So I left, I petted Hyménée, and then, in Maryse's bed, I fell asleep.

All the next day, I had no stories to tell. That evening mattered so much to us, Hyménée and me, as though we sensed that with the new stories from the curé, everything could change. And I went to Roger's door once more, which he opened for me right away this time, but in his cassock. And I think that I liked him better without it, as I'd seen him the night before, naked from the waist up and rather solidly built, because without his dreary clothes, we were more alike, him and me. Once again he offered me soup, and this time I ate it even though it was lukewarm and had too much pepper, but no one said anything at all. Afterwards, it was all quiet, I looked at my feet and Roger put another log on the fire, and I thought how pretty the light was. For me, my favorite color is orange. There was plenty of orange in the fire.

"So you came for a story, François?"

"Yes, Roger."

"What kind of story?"

"A story to tell together. For Hy—"

There I stopped short, because I couldn't tell Roger about Hyménée and me, that we were like a pair of tractor wheels, because he already thought I was completely bonkers.

"For going to the other side of the water, Roger."

There, I'd said it, just like that, to get myself out of a bad spot, and what had I done but get myself into another one, thinking of crossing the river without realizing it, me too, against the father's orders, and I thought to myself that now I was in for trouble. But Roger didn't get up, he didn't say, "So, you want to cross the river, François?" or, "So, you want to join Maryse, François?" or even worse, "Is it because of your mother, François?" which would have made me jump out the window again and race back home like a thief. No, Roger nodded his head and repeated, "The other side of the water, the other side of the water," as if he were searching for something in his head, while the fire crackled on. In a minute his eyes lit up and he said, "I think I have what we need, François," and he took from his bookcase a brown book and handed it to me and I took it and leafed through it: no pictures inside, no blond woman, no snake, nothing. I gave him a worried look. He said, "It's *The Inn of the Guardian Angel*, it's a beautiful story." That suddenly sent a chill up my spine, but Roger seemed excited, so I closed it and looked at my feet. And Roger began to tell his story. Not really tell it, he spoke as he looked at what was written in the book. Me, I didn't move, not a hair, just trying to keep it all in my head, to learn it by heart, so that I could go back and tell her, my Hyménée, what I'd heard. It started off well, this story, there was a man who discovered two children asleep under an oak tree with words that I didn't know, and I had to interrupt Roger so that he could repeat them to me, explain them to me, and so I could get those words into my head once and for all. Words like *bringing aid*, *devotion*, *pout* . . . very strange, very pretty words. After a while, I wasn't afraid of crossing the river anymore, or of the father, I no longer looked down at my feet but at Roger who was reading, then turning a page, then another, stopping to drink a little wine. Sometimes I stretched my leg or my arm, making no noise so as not to wake the children in the story or the soldier's dog, sometimes I added a log to the fire because the orange was threatening to disappear and that was no good. At one point Roger looked at his watch and said that it was getting late and that was all for tonight. "But the captured general?" I said. "What about the general?"

"I'll read you more another time."

"Tomorrow, Curé?"

"Tomorrow's no good, let's say next Monday."

"That's a long time, Curé."

"I can't do it before then, François."

So I set off again, cursing Roger a little for having so many things to do that took him away from our story of the guardian angel, Hyménée's and mine.

→>-<←

But in the end those five days passed quickly. More quickly than I imagined because I loved telling it to Hyménée, that story, starting it over and over again in the tall grass, inventing details that surely my Roger had forgotten to tell me, but also because on Saturday the father's knees began to give way and he couldn't stay upright at all, not even in his chair, so he ended up lying down. And me, I stayed with him just in case, not knowing what else to do, because Jules was on the tractor and Arthur on the road, so who else was there? I prepared everything for the pigs, food, water, and all of that. Hyménée knew the way to go, they could manage. All day long I stayed there beside the father, watching him sleep, holding the glass to his lips, wiping his forehead when it got damp, replacing the sheet when it fell and his hand, his sweaty hand, without squeezing it too hard. *Devotion*, as Roger had taught me, how it produced so much happiness and gratitude. He didn't speak, the father, he just said, "There was nothing else to do . . . ," opened his eyes a little, hardly at all, and then let his eyelids close again. I stayed with him like that for two days, and one morning when I put the spoon in his mouth, he said, "Maryse," looking at me as if he didn't see me anymore, and then I got really scared. I let the bowl drop and ran out onto the road shouting for my brothers, but they didn't answer, too far away for sure or else the wind carried my cries to the other side of the river, who knows, so I kept going as far as the house where old Lucie lived, who knew a bit about plants and seeds and who might have been able to save our Jean-Paul if it hadn't been too late. As I ran over the stones, I was hoping she'd be there in her garden picking herbs and not out on the road or at market shaking her saint medal and reading palms for a few coins. She was standing by the well, old Lucie, and when I came up behind her, she didn't even jump, she said, "It's you, François," and I didn't have to nod my head, she took my hand and leaned on my arm so that I could lead her with my eyes that could still see since hers were long gone. I had never been so close to her, pressed together like that, and it was funny to smell her, old Lucie, because she had the odor of the outdoors and the damp, like when you leave wood out in the rain too long and moss begins to grow on it. I didn't dare ask her how she knew it was me because I was afraid of making her angry, because with witches, it's better to have them in your pocket than chasing your butt. That lasted awhile, that walking arm in arm, because Lucie didn't move too fast, I'd never noticed her stiff leg, maybe because I didn't dare look at her on the road, on account of the evil eye and the stories I'd heard about her. When we arrived at the house, she stood up straight, she seemed to be sniffing all around her, and then she murmured, "It hasn't changed," and I wondered when she'd been here before because I'd never seen her here, never, and all of them, my brothers and father, they avoided Lucie on the road and they made fun of her stooped back, her wild hair, but never her eyes, blue as the sky and now fixed on me without seeing me. She said, "It was just after your birth," as if she had heard me in my head asking when she'd been here last, and I was scared, so scared that I almost peed my pants, and then she added, "You mustn't be afraid, François, not you, not you." She let go of my arm, she said, "Let me go, I know where it is," she grasped the handrail and suddenly she stood upright, and I watched her climb straight up the stairs, and at that moment I thought that just after I was born she had climbed them as well and maybe before that, and now it wasn't hard for me to imagine that she had once been young, beautiful, and blond before she'd been caught in the Saint John's Day fires, because right now she seemed light and full of light, so that it made me happy to watch her. Arriving at the top, she knocked on the father's door and murmured, "Jacques, it's Lucie," and in she went, just like that.

I didn't know what to do. I wanted to run to Hyménée and bury my face behind her ear where it's so soft, and at the same time I told myself that if I stayed there on the stairs or, with a little courage, behind the door, I might learn something about Maryse, Jean-Paul, a mother I must have had, and all those things no one talked about that sometimes kept me tossing and turning in my bed, over and over all night long. I took off my boots, I climbed that confounded staircase that creaked like the devil, and I balanced right on the edges where the steps weren't giving way under the weight of our heavy tread. Inching closer, I finally managed to press my ear right up against the father's door. At first I couldn't hear much of anything, because inside my body was shaken in all directions, and it was pounding, trembling, and knocking so loud that the noise inside drowned out the noise outside. So I closed my eyes, I ordered it to stop, and then I could begin to hear the words.

Words like, "That's in the past now," "There was nothing else I could do," which the father repeated again, and also, "You've got to tell him the truth, Jacques, or else it'll follow you to your grave." And then, "No, no, no," and then "Maryse" once, and then "Victorine," "Victorine," and "Victorine" again. And then their two voices rising, and the father yelling, "Get out of here, Lucie, I know you bring bad luck everywhere you go, I know you do!" She opened the door—I just had time to leap down the stairs, landing at the bottom again, so that they wouldn't know I'd heard all the words they'd said—and she replied, "It'll keep eating away at you, like it's eating away at you already, Jacques." And she took my arm and said, "Lots of water, you must make him drink lots of water, and then you must boil gentian and plantain leaves with cloves, four times a day, and you must give them to him with broth, and in a week, he'll be better." And then we walked to her house, pressed together, me in her odor of moss and with so many questions spinning in my head, like what was in the past now and who was Victorine and where was my Maryse, but fear weighed down my tongue and I looked down at the dust in the road the whole way. At the little rusty gate, Lucie let go, she sought my forehead with her hands, and she said, "Thank you, François, you're a good fellow," and I stood there like an idiot with my arms hanging at my sides and I watched her enter her house, feel her way along the wall, and then shut the door.

→>–◄–

It was Monday. The father had taken the broth, he was resting in bed, hands on the sheets, looking at the ceiling, the brothers were playing cards, so it was time for me to head to

Roger's. I had washed and dressed as for Jean-Paul's burial, because since Lucie, I was beginning to understand that you can't always stay filthy, or else you'll end up alone, even though you already are most of the time. He was standing in his kitchen, Roger. I knocked at the windowpane. He was taken aback for a moment, but I saw that he was glad to see me cleaned and combed. He said, "Well, my goodness, François," and I felt myself turn red as an apple in August. He had set the table for both of us, and I finished everything he laid out because I hadn't had much to eat since the father had gotten sick, no one made meals anymore, not my brothers or me. It was something like chicken, mushrooms, and potatoes. It was good. Afterward we cleared the table, Roger and me. We sat down, he took the book from the big bookcase, but before reading, he smiled at me and began his small talk.

"How are you, François?"

"Good, Curé."

"Did you have a good day, François?"

"Yes, Curé."

"What did you do, François?"

"The things I do, Curé, all the things I do."

"Tell me, François, can you tell me?"

"Well, Curé . . ."

But he kept smiling at me with a smile that broke my heart, so there I was beginning to tell him about the morning sun behind the clouds, foraging, and big old Médard who hurt his leg and the splint that I made with string and a piece of wood, and old Lucie's broth that I took to the father, since I had to tell about her, the one who smelled like moss, and her visit to the father, and how each time you had to make the father drink it because, ever since old Lucie left, he stared at the wall and he didn't say a thing except to wonder out loud if he'd be back on his feet in a couple days to count our money and figure out everything there was to be done here. I told him that this *devotion*, it wasn't as easy as in the book, and a smile rose in my Roger's eyes, so I went on. I told about my nap between Hyménée's legs and when I washed at the river and me running very fast to eat with you, Roger. And he listened to me, and when I finished telling, he opened the book, and we began with *The Inn of the Guardian Angel* again and made our way along the roads toward a great adventure while the candle on the table grew smaller and smaller. And then Roger closed his book and said, "Until Monday, François," and I wasn't afraid anymore because I knew that the week ahead would bring me back to Roger and the inn where the children were no longer abandoned.

→>-<←

It was then I decided to walk the streets of our village. Before, I had never done that, but now it was decided. It couldn't be done every day, only Sunday when our Arthur was out rambling and Jules was oiling his machines and the father was napping with a handkerchief over his face. I had only ever crossed through the village to do something in particular: go to Roger's, follow Jean-Paul's coffin, take the horse to the farrier's. So I had never seen the village for what it is: a village with a square and four roads that go in four directions. The first road is the one that leads to our house and stops short because of the river. The next two climb toward the hill with houses, not farms, houses. Some with flowers at the windows, others with laundry, some with nothing. And walking along these roads, I thought to myself that it was pretty, this village where I had a friend, Roger. The last road was the one to the cemetery and I didn't take that one. We'd been there once, the day when we'd lowered Jean-Paul into the ground. And the whole way back Maryse had been sniffling and since she didn't have a handkerchief she wiped her nose on her sleeve, and me, I didn't know what to do because I didn't have a handkerchief either, but I wasn't crying, I was looking at Maryse and her nose and her red eyes and I promised myself that I would never again set foot behind that gate where the bodies awaited their final journey, as if Jean-Paul had ever gone on journeys, Jean-Paul who had always stayed home.

What's nice about going for walks is that sometimes you pass people and then they greet you and you greet them, and it's a little like you're not a stranger anymore. That Sunday she was hanging her laundry by the side of her house. A lady. Big and fat with long brown hair. A flowered dress, blue shoes. When I passed, she said hello. "Hello," I said, "hello, Madame." She said, "It's a beautiful day."

"Yes," I said, "yes, it is."

"Where are you from?" she asked with a smile that showed all her teeth.

"From the farm at the end, by the river."

"The Sorrente farm?"

"Yes, that's where I'm from. I'm François Sorrente."

"I'm Amélie. Amélie Dufour. Nice to meet you, François."

She extended her hand so I had to take it, her hand, and it was warm, not soft, no, not soft, but warm, warmer than Lucie's arms, and it felt strange to hold it, so I let it go.

"We don't often see you in the village, you and your family," she added.

"Arthur, you must see him, he sells our hams and cheeses."

"Oh yes, I know him," she said with a smile, as if there was something to understand, and what it was I didn't want to know. "Would you like something to drink, François?"

"No," I said, "no, I'm in a hurry."

I was going to add, "Hyménée's waiting for me," but then she would have found out I was really bonkers, but maybe no more than she was, looking at me with her mouth open like I was a piece of fruit about to hit the ground.

"Good-bye, François."

"Good-bye, Madame."

"Amélie, you can call me Amélie. See you soon, François?"

And I went back home.

→>·<←

What I need, this is what I said to Hyménée, what I need is someone I can ask all these questions without being afraid, without getting caught. You understand that, Hyménée? She understood for sure. I could see it in her eyes: you can't drag your feet, François, any time that passes is time lost, François.

It was noon, the pigs were sprawled in the cool shade. No noise on the paths, I approached the shed. He was there, under the tractor, and that suddenly made me less afraid, seeing only his feet. I heard him breathing hard like someone fighting a giant. So I said, "Am I bothering you, Jules?" His feet jumped and then fell back with a loud bang.

"Jesus Christ, François, you scared the hell out of me, what do you want? What do you want, it's not like I've got anything better to do."

"You need help?"

"A little, I can't get this bolt loose."

I slid down beside him. It was completely dark. My brother, he smelled like the earth and sweat and also like straw. I concentrated hard, clenched my teeth, and in one try, the bolt came loose.

"Thanks, François."

"What was there beyond the river, Jules?"

"What do you mean, what was there?"

"Before."

"Before what? There wasn't anything, there isn't anything, you know that. You can see it yourself. Nothing, nothing at all beyond the river. Why do you ask that?"

"I want to know."

"You aren't going to do what your Maryse did, by chance?"

"Cut that out. I just want to know why the walls are all black, standing there like that for nothing. What were they before?"

"Before what?"

"Before they were all black, Jules, before that."

"I don't know, how do you expect me to know? They've always been black, that's all. Stop snooping around. Stop stirring up trouble. Take care of your pigs, that's all. I'll tell the father if this keeps up. You know what he said."

"I know, I know."

He didn't need to say it again. I raced right back to the pigs and I hid my face and I kept my distance from Hyménée so that Jules wouldn't discover us, so that he wouldn't think I'd gone bonkers over a sow who put ideas in my head, like that I might want to leave, and so that he wouldn't make her into ham just to teach me a lesson and to get my head screwed on straight.

That evening after supper I got out my sidekick with the mother-of-pearl buttons and I played some tunes. The one of the ass looking for its way, the one of the knight with the shattered armor returning from the Crusades along muddy paths, the one of the flower about to die for the love of a beautiful lady. And in the courtyard around the table and the bottle of wine, all of them, Arthur, Jules, and the father, they looked off in the distance and the worry lines left their foreheads. And sometimes I saw their legs under the tablecloth, humming along with my songs.

As I played, I wondered why it was that we were always alone, we Sorrentes, why no one ever visited except the girls after Arthur, who always left again once they'd let out their cries. The only one who had friends was me, with Hyménée and Roger and maybe Lucie, if she counted. In *The Inn of the Guardian Angel*, Moutier the soldier makes loads of friends. And here we were alone, all the time. Maybe books lie, maybe they do nothing but lie, so what's the use of reading, just to start hoping for things that won't ever happen. I also wondered if I loved them, my brothers and father. They were there, for sure, and always had been, and that was something at least. But love, like Maryse had told me in her song for sleeping, love you'd pine away for, love you'd climb a hill for, love that wore you out, I knew nothing about that. I'd loved Oscar for sure, and Maryse too, and maybe I still loved her because Maryse was still alive but on the other side. But sometimes I thought maybe I hadn't ever loved her since I hadn't left with her because of being scared of the father and the river.

→>−<-

The next day I decided to go right to the cemetery to see the mother I must have had. Because she wasn't hanging around some corner of the farm, for sure, she wasn't wandering the paths here, she had to be waiting for me in the ground. How come we hadn't thought of that, Hyménée and me? If she wasn't there, my mother, then she wasn't anywhere, anywhere at all. When Jean-Paul died, my eyes were too clouded over to think of it. Now I laughed with Hyménée, it seemed so simple to me. "In the ground! In the ground!" I cried, waving my arms and legs in the air, my stomach quivering with happiness because we seemed so close to our goal. All I had to do was go to Jean-Paul's grave and look around. I could see it in my mind's eye, his grave. Once I'd found her, my mother, I could talk to her, tell her everything I couldn't tell Maryse anymore, because she would see me, my mother, that's for sure, like the blond woman with the child on the farm who had risen straight to heaven.

I'd taken some charcoal from the stove and the paper we used to wrap our cheeses, since I didn't know how to recognize the words. I would copy out all the signs I found on the surrounding stones. On Monday, with my friend Roger, I would understand the signs and I would at least learn her name and her age, this mother about whom I'd once asked the father when I was no bigger than a spade, but he had only stared straight ahead as if night had fallen and it was time to turn out the lights.

I took the fourth road in the afternoon when everyone was resting. On the square I saw Amélie, who'd talked to me the other time. She gave me a little wave and a smile. I smiled back but I didn't stop because I didn't have much time. They couldn't find out at home that I was off wandering about the roads. It was still there, that cemetery, it hadn't changed a bit. The gate creaked, I saw the wide path ahead of me and all the little ones, and suddenly I realized this would be more complicated than I thought, finding our Jean-Paul again, because I'd been here only once and that was a long time ago, and if you don't know how to read you're like a blind man lost in the woods, and it would take endless cheese papers to cover the whole cemetery and sort it out with Roger, to find them, my brother and my mother as well. I wandered around a bit, but it was all gibberish, everything looked like everything else, and I didn't recognize anything. I felt like crying right out there in the open, but I stopped myself because the gate creaked and so I wasn't alone anymore. I didn't want to turn around because you could see it in my eyes that I was about to cry, for sure, and I didn't want anyone laughing at me or calling me a girl. I was afraid, too, that maybe it was someone from my family, so I stood up straight as a fence post, like I was watching some bird of prey, a buzzard or an eagle or a sparrow hawk, something you'd never see here, and like I hadn't come to find a tomb or to look at anything, really, what a ridiculous idea. But the gravel crunched slowly in my direction and I could tell that we were soon going to find each other on the same path. I could take off at full speed because I can run very fast, maybe you don't know it but when it comes to catching piglets, there's no one faster than me. But there was no use in that, because once the wolf catches you, you're caught, so I turned around and there she was again, Amélie, but not looking at all like when she'd smiled at me a little earlier. No, now she was dressed like a princess in a thin dress, high heels, and a straw hat that nearly hid her eyes. She was wearing makeup too, and she stood there, all big and fat in her dress, looking at me like she had something to tell me that I should have already understood. She flashed me a big smile and, not knowing anything, I smiled back. She looked me straight in the eye and said, "What are you doing here, François?" and her look bore down on me like the father's when he suspected I was hiding something from him. And I knew at once that I couldn't tell her anything, she was so caught up in what she wanted to do that there was no room inside her for my mother or even Jean-Paul though he was thin as a rail. So I said, "It's Roger."

"Roger the priest, François?"

"Yes, Roger the priest, Amélie. He asked me for something."

"What did he ask you for, François?"

"It's a secret. A secret, a secret of the dead, I can't say."

But she kept asking me questions, and I couldn't answer, and then she moved closer to me and I smelled her perfume, it was like roses but very strong, like crushed roses, a little rotten, like if you left them standing in water too long, and her mouth was crushed too, red like blood, and she was breathing hard, so hard, I didn't know what to do anymore and when she ran her hand through my hair I almost screamed in her face, screamed loud and pushed her against a cross and threw gravel at her, all the gravel on the path, but no, I had to stay calm in my head and my body, because what I wanted was to find the mother I must have had and if I acted crazy I wouldn't be able to come back to this cemetery, and no way was I going to let that happen, so I let her rummage around in my hair with her hand and then move down lower and then even lower. I couldn't tell if I liked that or not, it was the first time it had happened to me, I looked down at her hand, her fat hand with all its gold rings that was venturing toward my belt and then right into my pants.

Her work finished, she laughed a little and said, "Odd doing that in a cemetery." I pretended to laugh too, what else could I do? The sun had shifted far to the west, and I thought that nap time must be over at the farm and that the father would be expecting his broth and that I hadn't gotten anywhere, and that it was rotten luck, this Amélie, because I might have to come back at night, to the cemetery, to go about my business in peace. I blurted out that I had to get going, right now, and so good-bye, I stood back so as not to be touching her, because that was how I could be done with her as soon as possible, and because I didn't know what to do with her big body, but I saw that she didn't seem to like that, Amélie, her eyes turned black as the charcoal in my pocket, then she planted her lips on mine, alright, off you go before you get stuck here. I said thanks, thanks very much, and I took off like a madman, praying to high heaven that the mother I was going to find wouldn't be like Amélie but like the blond woman of the farm or Elfy or Madame Blidot who welcomed wayfarers at the Inn of the Guardian Angel and asked you, when they wanted to give you something, if you wanted it, and didn't come sneaking up behind you on the gravel path to do you in. All afternoon I could hardly breathe and my head was on fire. So I lay down between Hyménée's legs for some comfort and I could tell that she was disappointed too by the way things had gone at the cemetery since we'd believed we were so close to our goal, her and me. She tried hard to tell me stories. Beautiful stories to pass the time. But apparently not today because all afternoon, time hung still over us, not moving an inch.

That night the father asked me to play something to celebrate his health, his good health fully recovered. "And last night," I said, "what was that for?"

"That was for almost recovered, go on, François, play, play for your father who thumbs his nose at death, she'd better watch out, death, and Lucie, too, acting like she knows so much. Your father, he's laughing in her face. Play, François, play, we have to make her dance, we have to make her bleed tonight."

"I don't have the heart," I said before I even thought about it, "I don't have the heart."

"Play anyway, François."

"I don't want to, death scares me."

"I said play, what, are you deaf?"

So I went to find the accordion, because there was no standing up to the father, he was stronger, and even if I said no, sooner or later I'd end up having to back down. That evening my music was so full of gravel and cemetery paths you walked down only to come back emptier than a drum that he couldn't bear it, the father, and after three songs he said, "That's enough, François, what's wrong with you?"

"Nothing."

"You're as much fun as a hanged man tonight."

"There's nothing wrong with me."

"It wouldn't be a little heartache, would it?" said Arthur.

"A little what, Arthur?"

"A little heartache for big fat Amélie," and Arthur fell over laughing, and our Jules and the father behind him.

"The fat one, eh?"

Suddenly I wanted to do him in, my brother with his blond curls.

"Amélie, don't play stupid, François. I saw you."

Right then I felt myself turn white as our cheeses, or the paper we wrapped them in, my heart sank to my stomach and I saw Amélie's fat hand again feeling my body and leaving me nothing of my own.

"You should have seen him," laughed Arthur, "François, he was talking to Amélie on the hill road, last Sunday, he even helped her hang up her laundry, he was smiling at her, he wasn't in the dung with his pigs, hey François?"

My blood rushed back to my heart because this had

nothing to do with the cemetery, and I answered, "Lay off, Arthur, lay off."

"And she, she couldn't control herself anymore, oh, he's so charming, this François, even with the sows, they can't stay away from him, better than wrapping cheeses, isn't it, François?"

They were laughing, all three of them, laughing the way they laughed, and I saw their teeth ready to bite you, trembling like little bells, and I wanted to rip off their heads to make them stop so I could go find Maryse again, and visit Jean-Paul, and learn about the mother I must have had, because it was them, and their laughter, and my fear of them kicking my butt, that kept me there like a coward, on this side of the river, like a dumb, blind fool who couldn't move.

"Shut up, I don't want to hear it, Arthur. I don't want to hear anything."

And I got up with my sidekick and its mother-of-pearl buttons.

"Come on, don't get all worked up, we were just fooling around. Come on, come back, François, you can take a joke, you're seventeen after all. Are you going to go run to your curé, François?"

After that I couldn't hear him because I slammed the

door and raced up the stairs to lock myself in my room so that this day could be over as soon as possible.

→>-<+-

That Monday, when night fell, I raced like a squirrel to Roger's, but that wasn't a good day because he was busy again, and I had to wait for the next day, and a day is a long time to wait when you add it to all those days you've already waited.

But the next day there I was, and earlier than before, because with the days getting shorter, night came more quickly and I could take off sooner, my boots under my arm. He was a little upset, Roger, about the night before, he told me a whole long story full of mix-ups and problems, something about the doctor's wife, Sybille, and then her husband who had left and a story about a key that I didn't understand at all, but really I wasn't interested in under-standing it since all I wanted was to find Jean-Paul's grave again, and as for the rest of it, so what.

But I let him read me some of *The Inn of the Guardian Angel* anyway, so as not to hurt him, because he had already lit the candle on the table and the fire in the hearth and what could I say—that Sophie Rostopchine who told this story, she was really something, because at the beginning of the evening, it didn't interest me at all, that story, because of all the questions in my head, but after a page, I couldn't turn away from the captured general and the two children and Moutier the soldier and the inn and the poor beaten child named Torchonnet and. . . . But I couldn't give in or I'd be done for. So I shook my head and let out a cry, so frightening that my Roger jumped in his chair and fell back with such a stunned look that I wanted to laugh, you'd think I'd pissed right in his kitchen just for the fun of seeing him turn that color. But this was no laughing matter, without a second thought, I blurted out my question, just so he'd get it into his head that this was serious, what I was asking him.

"I need to learn to read, Roger."

"Why, François?"

Well I thought that his question was idiotic, but I saw his face going all white again after being green, so I was gentle with Roger. Because he was my friend, and with friends in this world you have to take care of them, seeing as you never know just how long your life could last and especially since it can last a long time.

"Because, Roger. I want to know how."

"You could go back to school."

"No way, Roger. I'm too old, plus the father would

never allow that. He'd shut me up in the barn or kill me. Please, Roger."

"Why me, François?"

"Because you're a curé, Roger."

"It's not only curés who know how to read."

"Yes, but you won't laugh, you won't ask questions, I wouldn't be afraid to talk. And plus your soup is good, Roger, and I've had enough of being stupid and bonkers."

"I don't know if . . ."

"I can pay you if you want. I can help you out. Like your shutter there, I could fix it if you want."

"Alright. But one day a week, I can't do more."

"Thank you, Roger."

"Don't thank me yet. One night a week won't be enough, you'll have to work on your own. It won't be a piece of cake."

"I'm not scared. I'm done with being an idiot."

That evening we did the vowels, there are six of them. In *Jean-Paul Sorrente*, there are seven vowels, that's what Roger told me. In *Maryse*, three. In *maman*, two, but they're the same, so maybe that only makes one. But even though I learned all that, I can't go back to the tombs, because I need the consonants, the consonants are important, Roger says, without them, there's nothing. So I have no other choice but to wait, but that's better anyway because that's all the more time for Amélie to forget about me, and it'll be a while before I could stay calm watching her rings.

→>—<←

It was colder now. I hardly took the pigs out anymore because with all that rain and wind, if it keeps up, you're ready for the grave. I don't have much use for winter. It's the spring I like best, for sure. Because everything is bright and possible then. In winter you go deep inside of everything, and everything that happened the seasons before stays alive in your head. And all you can do is pile on more and more sweaters to try to warm up your heart.

In winter I had my tasks to do, like sealing up the windows of the house and cleaning the big rooms, because we were living inside it now, and our house needed its bath like everyone else, and scrubbing the clothes since in summer you went around half-naked with the brothers, but now you needed layers, and also making the meals. Cooking had mainly been Maryse's role, and now I liked taking it on, because since I'd started studying with Roger, Maryse's big cookbook wasn't just a ghost anymore but an object that could become my friend. And the idea even occurred to me that, for Christmas dinner, when I'd finished my alphabet, I could cook us a stuffed turkey like she used to, before life came crashing down on us.

I had begun walking into the village again. I set off down the paths about five o'clock, at dusk, when it's too dark for you to tell the difference between dog and wolf anymore. At that hour, everyone was at home and I was free to look inside the houses, to see how families lived when they were real families, not like at our house where there's endless silence because too many of us are gone. I was sure that I wouldn't run into Amélie because when night falls that scares the pants off women. I took the three roads, never the fourth one that leads you know where, because I still didn't have enough consonants and I didn't want to take the chance of botching things up again.

The road I took most often was the one leading straight up the hill where the houses had no flowers in their windows at the moment, but the care there, the presence, felt good, the *devotion*, as I had learned in Roger's book. There was also a spot where there was nothing along the road, only bushes and stones. Sometimes I stopped there, and I would sit down and light a match to a few twigs to warm my hands. I couldn't stay long, because the meal had to be ready to eat at seven, even if I made it ahead of time by getting up before dawn or using last night's leftovers. Sometimes when I sat dreaming too long on my hill, I woke with a start and ran all the way home, arriving out of breath, covered in mud, and completely done in.

It was a Tuesday, I remember, because the night before I had learned the *v* at Roger's and I thought of all the words that gave me now, like the words for bicycle, car, speed, life: *vélo, voiture, vitesse, vie*, and also the verbs *to come* and *to see*: *venir, voir*, all those things that are beautiful and good and that begin with *v*. I felt light and happy as well to know that I was reaching the end of the list of consonants, because after *v*, you only had three more letters since the *y* I already knew. I had decided to rest between two bushes when I heard Roger's voice. That brought joy to my heart because Roger is my friend, even if he's stiff as an umbrella, knows everything better than me, always makes me the same soup (carrot-cabbage), and spends his days in his infernal house.

But before I could call out to him that I was there, I heard another voice, so now I knew he wasn't alone, there was someone with him. I thought that in a minute he would be done with that person and it would be my turn, that's why I stayed there not moving. I didn't want to listen to what they were saying to each other, but my ears opened in spite of myself and after two minutes I understood that

I would have been better off anywhere but there, and now I really couldn't move, not so much as a fly, not so much as a fart, and most of all, everything I'd just heard, I must never breathe a word of it to anyone, no matter who, no one, not even to the walls of my room, which might repeat the sound of it.

It was a woman talking to him, my Roger, a woman with a gentle voice mingled with sighs and sniffling, and I imagined she was beautiful, of course, with long blond hair as well, even though I couldn't see a thing. It seemed like her head was all muddled with a whole heap of things and also that she'd been late because she was saying, "Even though I'm like a clock, my love, a clock," and she was scared, really scared. And my Roger, he didn't say anything much, not even, "It'll be alright," like when I sat shaking my head because I kept stumbling over hard words like the words for finger: *doigt,* or for heart: *coeur,* so the woman said to him, "What are you thinking, say something, my love, say something to me, don't leave me, my love," more and more loudly, and Roger, he didn't know what to do, so he went, "Shhh," he whispered, "Hush, Sybille, hush, someone might hear us," and the woman answered, "I don't care if someone hears me, I don't care, I don't care about anything now," so my Roger started to raise his voice, saying that she was crazy, completely crazy, "That's all bullshit," and I heard noises, like when bodies knock into each other, not wanting to hold each other or to let go and upset each other, then some dull sound, and I understood that my Roger had gone and that she was the only one left, her head against a bush, her hands in the dirt maybe, where else? I didn't dare move and at the same time I wondered if I shouldn't go rest my hand on her forehead, as so often at night I wished someone would come stroke my hair when I was lost in grief.

So, quietly I jumped to my feet and found myself beside her, she seemed to be eating the dirt and the grass, and I tried to rest my hand on her, but she understood nothing, she gave a start, she struggled and began to scream, "Let me go, let me go," I said, "It's for your grief, your grief, Sybille," but she didn't hear, she struggled harder and suddenly something in me wanted to squeeze her tight to make it stop, her loneliness and mine there in the dirt and the high grass, squeeze her so it would all end at once, and it was so big, what I felt at that moment, that suddenly I had to clear out of there, it made me afraid, the terrible thing that could happen, that I might smash her face with a rock, or that I might wring her neck, like when you want to finish off the hens, or that with one stroke I might bleed her like a pig when its time comes, and I guessed that wouldn't do either of us any good and it would put an end to all our projects, Hyménée's and mine, so I let go of her and she started to quiet down a little. I raced home, top speed, and I could tell as soon as I reached the door that the roast was burned and the vegetables worse than death warmed over, and I'd better come up with an excuse fast to escape the wrath of the three waiting for me at the kitchen table.

Climbing into bed, I couldn't help hearing my Roger's voice when I closed my eyes, like when I drag my pigs to the courtyard to bleed them out, when they smell it and they know that this is it, no way out, none, and I was thinking of the woman who called him "my love" and maybe I'd been wrong, maybe he did know something about love, my curé, and maybe it was better that way because everyone deserves to know it at least once in your life, the love that gives you the courage to get up in the morning, like me with Hyménée, or with Maryse, before that all went to the dogs.

The next Monday, my Roger looked like soup that's been sitting on the windowsill for three days, that bubbles all by itself, and if you swallow it by mistake, you're not a pretty sight. In any case, there wasn't any soup.

"Didn't have time, François."

"It doesn't matter, Curé."

"How are you, François?"

"Pretty good, Curé. You?"

"Could be better."

It was obvious that his head was all turned around, seeing as he hadn't shaved, his nails weren't cut, and the open bottle beside his glass was half-empty. That evening I learned nothing at all, because my Roger, he couldn't remember the last consonants anymore, or *The Inn of the Guardian Angel*, nothing at all, he stared at the candle in the middle of the table, sighed, and ran his hand over his forehead, then he rested his head in his hands and then it was like I no longer existed, his back heaving with sobs, my Roger, then when the candle went out and the bottle had long been empty, I put him on my back, the curé, I climbed the stairs and tossed him into bed.

I understood well enough that I wasn't going to get anything at all out of Roger. It was almost Christmas, meaning that the fields were freezing over and I was still missing three letters from the alphabet. I had to find them if I wanted to make the stuffed turkey, then I had to get to the cemetery to see our Jean-Paul again and start a new year that wouldn't be such a waste as the one just ending. I thought of old Lucie, but she couldn't see a thing, so there was no one left but her. It sent a shiver up my spine just thinking of her rings and her hands that knew a thing or two, and then her flesh that spilled out and the folds of her belly when she sat down, and also that she was much older than me, even though she colored her hair, but I could see that some of it had no color, and the roots too. And then too I didn't know how to go back to her again, seeing as I'd taken off like that, because I'd kept clear, and after her visit to our house, I'd never gone back there. Flowers, that was a good idea, but in the middle of December, you couldn't find any under the frost and ice. There was also holly or fir boughs, but I don't know why, it seemed strange to me to offer them to a woman, things that scratch and sting, even if she only half pleases you, even if you're resigned to her dirty work. Finally, I settled on an apple cake—that, I decided, was a good idea.

→►◄←

When she opened the door, I could tell she had a hard time believing that here I was, after waiting for me for days on end. She glanced up without looking directly at me, "Well, see who it is."

"Hello, Amélie," I said.

"Well, don't just stand there. Come in, François."

She took my coat. Her house wasn't at all like Roger's or old Lucie's. There were things everywhere. Cartons, mirrors, cushions, fabric, candles, bows, lace. She repeated, "Come in, François, come in," but in the midst of all that, I didn't know where to put my body. Finally I sat down on a chair she showed me, behind the table. She sat down on the other side.

"So, it's been a while, François."

"I brought you an apple cake."

"Thank you."

She put it on the chair beside her without taking any notice of it, and she looked right at me. Directly at me.

"And otherwise, François?"

"I'm good. And you, Amélie, how are you?"

I didn't know where to look anymore. I thought what a stupid idea it had been, to come see her like this, that I would never have the courage to ask her about the last three consonants I needed, and I saw them, her fingers covered with rings that moved across her forehead, her hair, and then into the hollow of her shirt to straighten her collar, and then rose and slid across the table, and then without my even thinking about it, it came out, just like that.

"What is there on the other side of the river, Amélie?"

"There's nothing there, François."

"There is, too. The burned buildings."

"Oh that. The Bridge Farm. That was a long time ago. It must have burned down sixteen, seventeen years ago, maybe."

"How did it happen?"

"No one knows. It happened at night, the wind was blowing hard. It went up like a torch. Even the wooden bridge was gone."

"Did anyone get out?"

"No one. They all died. Old Martin and his two sons, the daughter-in-law, and even the little one who had just been born. Why are you asking this?"

"Just to find out. No one ever talks about it at our house."

"Is that why you came to see me, François?"

I looked down so that she couldn't see how red I was turning.

"No, of course not, no. Just to see you, Amélie. To see you."

"You know, I came by the farm a while ago. Did anyone tell you?"

"Uh . . . no. They didn't tell me."

"And the letter? I sent you a letter. At least you got that, the letter?"

"The . . . I didn't get anything, Amélie. Nothing at all. In any case . . . I still can't read very well, I'm just learning how, even though I know almost all of the letters in the alphabet."

At that she smiled, as though reassured, she got up and came toward me, opening the buttons of her shirt, and I understood that now wasn't the time for the last three letters, but that didn't matter because I had already learned about the other side of the river and I also knew that I could come back to Amélie's whenever I wanted now, no matter what time it was, even without cake.

→>-<+

I got back home just before the sun rose, without making any noise or commotion, and that was good, because a little later, Jules banged on my door like when Jean-Paul had fallen off the roof and that scared me, and he said, "Get up in there, you're going to have to go to market instead of Arthur who can't." And it was clear why he couldn't go, Arthur, just looking at his face, all blue and smashed, and his jaw, which had doubled in size. He had turned a sickly gray, because it was something, the beating he'd taken, and I heard him hissing between his teeth, "What can I do about it, what can I do?" So I made some very black coffee and I gave a cup to my brother all collapsed in his chair, and then Jules and me, we carried him up to his bed, and he was moaning, "My head, my head." So I made him drink half a bottle of whiskey, and that sent him off to sleep better than any of old Lucie's remedies, I think. I loaded up our cheeses and set off down the road in the van. I had almost never driven it alone. Sometimes around the courtyard just for fun, or to park it in the shed when my brother had something else to do. The road to market was perfectly straight, so there was nothing to worry about. I loved the noise it made when you drove fast, on account of the missing back window, which our Arthur had replaced with plastic. The cheeses smelled good too, and the ham and sausage. The eggs didn't smell like anything much, but they were there. I was a little tired after the night's sleep I'd missed, and I sang Maryse's song because it would be a disaster for sure if I ended up driving it into the ditch, our old van, for a night spent beside Amélie.

→>-<←

I was all set up at market, and, well, I was pretty pleased with my little shop. And when our Roger went by on his bicycle, he stopped short and said, "Oh! François!" and I could see it in his eyes that my friend was happy to see me. He asked why I didn't come visit him anymore, he missed our evenings together and he made that soup only for me because, all by himself, he didn't feel much like cooking. He bought two cheeses, one with pepper and one with herbs, which I wrapped in paper, then put in a bag, adding two eggs because I was happy to see him, I even said to myself that maybe, maybe I would set foot in his house again, even though my Roger was still not really back on track yet, that was clear enough by how thin his face looked and how his eyes seemed to be sunk into their sockets. I kept on selling my goods and I felt proud because my stall, it was never empty, not in the least, and someone even complimented me on my smile and my manner and sometimes I slipped a little parsley between the sausages, just like that, in the bottom of the bags, just for the pleasure of it. And when I saw old Lucie go by with her saint medal to tell all the good luck and all the bad luck that would soon befall us, I slipped some cheese into her bag, discreetly, because there's no doubt about it, it's no picnic to still be wandering the roads when you're old and full of woes, and also because of the evil eye, which I really wanted to avoid. Once in a while I looked up and saw my Roger, still there, on the bench in the square, a little hunched over, as if he were waiting for something to happen. Sometimes he took a sip of his beer, which always seemed to be the same one, but thinking about it, you don't have to be a curé to understand that he was doing himself in, my Roger. At some point, pity overcame me, so I asked Marcel, who had the vegetable stall across the way, to watch mine for me, and I went to fetch him because it was so hard to see my friend like that, collapsed on his back now, his legs sprawled. I propped him against my arm to help him over to the back of the van where he could sleep it off. We crossed the square, his head knocking against my shoulder, and I thought, this is my Roger, who read me *The Inn of the Guardian Angel* by that Countess of Ségur, who told me there was always a place for abandoned children with no one to love them, with nothing; that the sun also shone on them and there was jam and fresh bread; that there was a bed where you could rest and a smile awaiting you when you woke. We kept to the side of the road, Roger and me, like a dilapidated castle about to fall to pieces. I looked to the left and to the right. I didn't see any cars at all, so I took a step forward, my leg bearing all the weight of my friend, his eyes closed, his breathing like when a horse is trying to blow all the air from its nostrils because it can't stand it any-more, and then I saw her, the woman, or rather she was the one looking at us, him and me. And in her blue eyes, blue like the river I would never cross, I felt her terror, ice-cold, and saw her turn on her heel and take off running, fast, as fast as her legs could carry her, in her flowered dress that blew in the wind, and I understood suddenly that she was the one, the one in the night, whose forehead I'd touched, who'd pushed me away crying, "Let me go, let me go."

I didn't get a good look at her, like anything you happen upon unexpectedly, and that disappears before you know it. That night, slipping into Maryse's bed, I tried to remember the woman who had called Roger in the dark "my love, my love." She had blond hair, tied back, but surely it came loose sometimes, she had blue eyes like roadside flowers, like Maryse's forget-me-nots, a long neck, a thin nose, and she ran like a doe runs, she runs although it's already too late, a bullet can go so much faster, so much farther, and it'll leave a trail of red down her neck.

As for Roger, I laid him down in the back of the van on a piece of cardboard. I put some water on his handkerchief and I moistened his temples, like that, gently, I wanted to smooth his hair to make him presentable, well-groomed, the way he was on his bike when I still used to see him mornings when the sun rose early. I arranged his hands and I saw that there was blood under his fingernails and that it couldn't be easy staying all alone like that in his big house.

I couldn't stay long, because Marcel, he hadn't even known me yesterday, hardly even today, he barely knew me from Adam, or Eve, or anyone. So I went back to my stall, I kept selling and selling, and by the end of the morning, when I saw Amélie, I had almost nothing left, so I gave her some eggs, and Marcel too, because they had each given me something, each in their own way, and so, when I drove back in the empty van, I didn't even have to move my Roger, to wedge him in beside the sheep cheeses. I even had room for his bike. I drove right to the presbytery, poured water over my friend's head, and sang Maryse's song to him, gently, softly, while I waited for him to come back, because he was going to come back someday, for sure, you come back, you always come back, that's a fact.

I watched him asleep in his bed and I looked at the sheets, rumpled, a little gray; his bedroom floor was covered with cigarette butts, the ashtrays were overflowing, there were papers and clothing everywhere. Outside, the winter light made shadows that danced on the wall. I heard birds singing and suddenly I thought of Hyménée and I told myself how lucky I was to have someone who understood me and that maybe that's what Roger needed, a pig like mine, who didn't ask anything of you, who was there for you, just her snout against yours. I didn't dare move and at the same time I was all set to smile at him, so that he would see it first thing, my smile, when he opened his eyes, Roger, because a smile makes all the difference, with a smile you're not alone anymore.

But when he opened his eyes, he started bawling like a baby, because it did him good to see me, even if I was stupid and a simpleton, he said, because he preferred the company of people like me, simple like me, to that of people who always know it all and think they're so just, because the just and the smart and the proud and the hypocritical ones he couldn't stand anymore, he preferred the company of people like me whose heads were full of air, because at least they were true. And me, I didn't know what to say when he squeezed my hand and smiled from deep within his eye sockets, I could only say "yes," because for as long as I can remember I've felt that deep within I really am stupid and a simpleton, because the father tells me that, because my fingernails are black, I live among pigs, and my life is so small—how can your life be big when you don't know how to read and you don't know anything but your village and Hyménée and Amélie and you, Roger, you?

→>-<←

When I got home to the farm and I saw their faces at the kitchen table, I understood that it had been a terrible day. It was already dark. Arthur's face wasn't black-and-blue anymore but grayish purple, and his arm was jammed into a sling. The father gazed out the window in silence and Jules looked down at his feet. They didn't ask where I'd been, what I'd been doing, how much money I'd made, any of that. There they were, as they'd always been, and I reheated the soup. They gulped it down, all three of them, Arthur making painful little whimpers each time he moved his jaw. No one said a word, I cleared the table in silence, then did the dishes, and afterwards, I lay down between Hyménée's legs and told her about my day, because for the last few days life had been moving awfully fast, and if you don't tell it to someone, you don't understand it anymore.

Hyménée listened to me as only she knew how, and then she told me about the day's grass, and the dew, and Daisy who's jealous of her and spends her time trying to find her, to drag her into the mud, and Hyménée tries to pay no attention to that "because she's a poor wretch, because she's ugly and no one loves her, and I shouldn't let her bother me," but there are times when Hyménée can't control herself, "You want to clout her, that sow, that dirty sow, so when you shove her against the barbed wire, a kind of joy rises in your gut, even if it's wrong, that kind of joy and pleasure from seeing her stumble on stones or get mounted by big old Médard, which no one likes." I suspected that it was doing something to her, Hyménée, that I was away more and more often, because that was no life for her, that one. I tried to reassure her, to say that nothing had changed, but I wasn't telling the whole truth that night, because I was beginning to feel that, with the letters I was learning, it was as though a new road lay before me and I could follow it only by myself.

→>-<←

The next day the father told me to wash down the farm from top to bottom because there was going to be a wedding here before long, and he said it in such a nasty way, with such a scowl, that you'd think it was a funeral. So I acted like I didn't want to know any more about it, I took the brush and pail and I scrubbed and scrubbed. There were stones to scour, beams to scrub, windows to wash; I've never been afraid of work because while the body slaves away, the mind can wander, and my mind had heaps of things to think about. I also thought to myself that sooner or later someone would tell me what was going on in this house, someone would tell me or be forced to tell me, nothing to get all worked up about. I started with the entrance and then the kitchen, filthy, so filthy. Then the parlor, and it was strange to go in there, because no one ever went into that room. A parlor is where you receive guests, and at our house, you couldn't really say we saw much of high society. It was gloomy with dust and things seemed abandoned, like in Maryse's room, except I did go in there to look after it. There was an old book open on the hearth, two half-burned logs, half-full glasses, old papers, and suddenly I thought to myself that this was the room where you could celebrate it, Christmas, with a turkey and chestnuts and maybe it wasn't too late, there were two weeks left and Amélie, she would give me the last three letters for sure, on account of the eggs that I'd slipped into her bag and the way she had smiled. That made me happy, that thought, so I started really slaving away so that everything would be clean, opening the shutters that always stayed closed, letting in fresh air, until that room didn't seem the same anymore. There were only the ashes in the hearth to get rid of and when I took the small brush to it, I heard a strange sound, like when you knock two pans together, and way in the back I saw a small metal box, covered with soot, which must have fallen into the fire some time ago. I pulled it from its dusty corner, polished it a little, and I was about to open it when all of a sudden I heard the door creak and I hid the box under my knee, you never know here, you have to be on your guard. Here it's better if you do things on the sly. I turned around fast and there was Arthur with a cloth wrapped around his chin and honestly, the way he looked, you'd never think that he made girls drop like flies.

"I can't stand it anymore. My head is going to explode."

"You want me to make you some tea, Arthur? That might help."

He followed me into the kitchen. I made him sit down in a chair and I bathed his forehead, temples, and jaw with a little well water, cold as ice, to anesthetize his pain. Then I went looking for restharrow roots at the edge of the lawn, rinsed them off, and started boiling water. I was thinking all the time about the metal box that I'd had to leave under the small case where the good glasses were kept; what if someone found it? Arthur would leave me in peace as soon as he'd drunk my tea, and then I could open it and find out what was in it because it didn't seem to be empty, that box. I imagined all the things it might hold, like jewels, papers, pearls, shells, or even hair, and during that time I didn't even hear my brother opening his mouth and talking to me, talking, talking like when you're on the verge of suffocating.

"I was the strongest," he was saying, "the strongest, but when five of them corner you, when two of them are holding your legs and two are holding your arms, what can you do, François, even if you're strong as the devil, there's nothing you can do, nothing you can do. And I don't even remember her anymore, not at all. Whether she's blond or brunet, if she's short or tall, I don't know. She has only herself to blame. I didn't want anything from her, it could have been anyone, it didn't matter. When I want something, I take it, and then afterwards, that's it, it's over. But they're talking about dishonor, and doing her wrong, and how her life is ruined. Well, what about mine? I don't want to get married. What does that bring you? Misery, that's all. Just look at the father and mother, that's what Jules said, that was a bad business. You, you never knew her, the mother. Me, hardly at all. Always looking across the river, that's what Jules told me, always quiet, never a smile, not a word, nothing, not a thing. So I don't want to get married. To live together just to end up old and sad? But they swore they'd break my arms and legs if I didn't take her. 'We're an honorable family,' they said. 'I don't love her,' I said. 'Who cares, you're going to marry her, Fanny, whether you like it or not.' So there it is. I'm sure she doesn't want to either. But we've got no choice. And she better not try asking me to account for myself, I'm not going to change my life one bit, it'll be just like before."

He went on and on, my brother, repeating the same things, and I wondered what she would be like, the one he didn't get to choose. Would she have blond hair too? Would she sing songs? Would she ask, "How was your day, Fifi?" I'd also heard what he'd said about the mother I must have had, whose name might have been Victorine—I really like the name Victorine, for a mother—who was never happy and who also looked across the river where the father didn't want anyone to go. Then I said to myself that my life is like a forest where there's no light, where I'm walking all by myself, and sometimes, with a forgotten word or phrase— because no one knows, even if I stay on this side, lost in my head all day long, I'm looking for them, the mother I must have had and my Maryse, and I haven't forgotten Jean-Paul either—it's as though a clearing suddenly appears and gives me the strength to keep looking, over and over again, because someday there won't be any more trees and I won't be afraid anymore, I will have reached a meadow full of flowers and that's when I'll know that I'm saved.

I made him drink so much restharrow-root tea, my Arthur, that afterwards, all he wanted to do was piss, piss, piss, and he took off in a hurry, and I saw my chance to get out of there with the metal box. I headed for the far meadow, slipping through the hole in the fence I'd made for Oscar and sticking close to the river, behind the bushes, where no one can see you. It didn't want to be opened, that box, which, before the fire, must have been ever so beautiful. When you wiped off the soot, you could see something like flowers engraved there, but so small and colorless, and it seemed like a box for a woman because flowers, they're for women, even though I myself like them in the fields, when they move with the wind, so much freer than we are. But me, I'm bonkers, an airhead, like my Roger said. I had to go back to the kitchen and get a knife, so set was the box on guarding its secrets, but finally I managed it and the hinges split apart like a moth in a flame. It was full of photographs, square with wavy white edges that rippled when you ran your finger over them. There was one of a little girl in front of a house, she was smiling and beside her was a dog, almost as tall as she was. There were others with an older girl with two braids and a smile, no dog, but the same house. She wasn't especially beautiful, that girl, not tall or short, just average, but she was calling to you from the photo as if to say hello, and even if you didn't know her, you wanted to stop and say hello to her. There were other photos with no people in them at all, nothing but trees or sheep or pigs (that one I liked a lot). Then there was a photo of the woman all in white with a bouquet, and that one, for sure, had to be the wedding, and suddenly she seemed as beautiful to me as the blond woman of the farm, but there was no one beside her, or maybe, since the photo was smaller, the man beside her had been forced out of it, and I wondered who could have been beside her and I was truly bonkers to ask myself that question, truly idiotic, because if this was the mother I must have had, then the one who must have been holding her arm, whose hand you could still see a little, that could only have been the father, and that seemed unimaginable to me, that he could have gotten married, lived with a woman, slept in the same bed with her, the father I'd only ever known to be alone, speaking only if he really had to, rough, sullen, and distracted, but it all must have happened, since here I am.

There were other photos, and those photos made me sick at heart and in my gut because there you saw her, the woman, with Maryse, Jules, Jean-Paul, and Arthur. You saw all five of them holding hands and smiling. And Maryse was beautiful with her braids, and Jules wore a shirt that had been ironed, and our Jean-Paul didn't look at us with that sad smile but proudly, holding his little bag like a man, and Arthur had no teeth yet at all, and about him was the air of someone who knows happiness and warmth and the arms of a mother. There were no photos with me. I turned the box upside down twice and nothing, nothing, nothing. It was as if no one had seen me come into that life, those arms, as if I'd arrived through the window, without warning, and no one had seen it happen. And I felt something dropping in my belly for a long time, as if there were a deep, deep hole and never again would I see the light. I wanted to throw the box into the river and die, die right there and then. But I stopped myself because a mother, that's something sacred, and Maryse too, especially Maryse, whom I missed suddenly, in my head and heart, in my forehead and shoulders where she leaned her head gently against mine with exhaustion. Because at the farm, she had been worn out from work, our Maryse, and sometimes in the evening you could see her legs trembling and she would need to sit down so as not to fall down, because she would go very pale suddenly, so I would lean all my weight against her body so that she could let her head drop without hurting herself, without coming to harm, because harm, if you don't watch out, it comes from everywhere.

I slipped through the fence again, the box held tightly under my sweater. I raced up to my room and tossed it under my socks in the wardrobe, where no one would think to look. Then, when I needed to think about everything that was going around in my head, I would have those photos, and even on those nights when you need to see the stars shining but the sky is all dark, I would be able to see them again, my Jean-Paul and my Maryse, gone now for such a long time.

I didn't stay down for long because of the cleaning, there was no lack of it to do. Oh no! The stairs, the kitchen, our bedrooms, and the father's. And even if it was hard work, it did me good to scrub, to wash, to stay bent over the dusting and the laundry, because without you knowing it, that gave you the sense that maybe you could start a new life. Because when you clean everything around you, it's as though you are cleaning inside you. It's bound to happen. I also went over Maryse's room and I left some wildflowers there, to say that someone was waiting for her here, if someday she got the idea of coming back.

That evening, we all ate in silence, the brothers and the father and me. There was only the creaking of a shutter, and when it came time for the fruit, the father said, "It'll be set for next week, Arthur. For next week."

"I couldn't care less," he said. "I won't get dressed up for it. I'll go like this."

"You can do whatever you want, so long as they calm

down, those crazy fools. I don't want any more trouble, you understand? I don't want to hear anything about your problems. And once she's here, your wife, she's all yours, because they can ruin your life just with their ideas."

Arthur shrugged his shoulders.

"What is she going to do here?" I asked.

No one answered, so I repeated the question louder, just to understand how this would all work now.

"Well she won't be sitting on her thumbs," said Jules, "we won't have anyone lazing around. She'll do the cooking and the laundry. You, François, you'll keep going to market. Arthur's had it. He's going to stay home for a while. And then no one loses out, you did a really good job selling last time."

I couldn't keep from smiling, because Jules has never been one for compliments. And then too, I liked the idea of it, being out on the roads, selling our cheeses, eggs, and hams.

→>-<←

But me, I didn't want to go to Arthur's wedding like that. Because I would be seeing my Roger and all the people from market there, who could maybe become my friends someday. I wanted them to smile when they looked at me and find me pleasant and well-groomed. Dressed in blue or gray, like Moutier in the book, who I'm not. Even Amélie, I wanted her to look at me, even though she hardly existed for me, or only when I felt alone, because I didn't know what to call what we did together, whether I liked it or didn't like it, this thing that I hid, like everything of mine, so that in the end you don't even know if it exists for real. The problem with Amélie was that there was Hyménée and I didn't want to be divided in half, even though I was beginning to understand that I wasn't an animal entirely and so there was something impossible about my sow and me. Maybe too, Hyménée, with her snout that could turn up truffles, already understood our situation, like a field you won't be sowing anymore, and that was the reason for her sad eyes when I lay down between her teats.

I didn't know if it was the fault of the books, this change in me, or the letters, or the photos, or simply the visit from old Lucie. It was impossible to go back to the way I was before, even if I had wanted to. Just like if I'd gotten it into my head to make the river flow in the opposite direction, to make it go back to its source, that would be completely bonkers, right? But Hyménée I would always love, for her gentleness, for her smell that did me good, for the times she stayed at my side when there was no one else. I'm not willing to forget that. I'm not.

→━◄━

Marcel was a little taller than me, a little heavier too, but I thought that with a belt it could work, I could look like Moutier from *The Inn of the Guardian Angel* as I imagined him. So when I saw him at market again, Marcel, his stall across from mine, I gave him a smile as bright as the sun, and when things slowed down and the shelves were getting empty, I left my cheeses and stood leaning against his booth on account of my bright idea that I wanted to run by him.

"My brother's getting married," I said.

"Yeah, I know," he said, scratching his ear, "he was asking for it."

And then he didn't say anything else. He watched the people going by and I didn't think he saw what was coming next, my idea.

"I don't have anything to wear, Marcel. I don't want to be a dirty slob that day."

"Your father can't do anything for you, with all his money? Some old clothes, that's no big deal."

"Doesn't seem like it. Especially since Arthur doesn't

want anything to do with his own wedding. Couldn't you lend me something so I won't look like a crazy lout?"

"We're not built the same, you and me."

"Yeah, I know that, but with a belt . . ."

"That won't work, François. But I've got an idea. My sister might have something for you."

"I don't want to go dressed like a girl, Marcel."

"Relax, you silly idiot. My sister's husband, rest his soul, was about your size. My idea's that if you had a little chat with my sis, she'd let you try some of his clothes."

"I'd be careful with them."

"That would be good, though I'm not sure it matters much anymore."

So that evening I stopped by Marcel's with the van, he hopped in, and we drove straight to his sister's. She lived in a house almost at the end of the other village, and a dog started barking when you pulled up and someone lifted the curtain at the kitchen window to see who you were. Marcel's sister's hair was all white and she stood there with her arms hanging at her sides as though she were all worn out, but her house smelled like cooked apples, so you knew even so she kept herself busy. I'd brought some goat cheese in my sack, so that each of us would get something out of this. Marcel explained our business. She shook her head in silence, looking down at the rug, and that lasted a good long while, so that I was thinking it was a lost cause and I was about to go home empty-handed. But finally she cleared her throat. "You know where to look," she said to Marcel, and up the stairs we went.

We entered the bedroom. Over the big bed with only one pillow, there was a photo of the deceased, well-groomed, with hair smoothed down and eyes that shone. He didn't look unpleasant, Marcel's brother-in-law, I even liked him and I thought to myself how sad death was when it took you before your time. I couldn't help asking Marcel what had happened to him, to Jeannot, as he was called.

"He died in service."

"What do you mean, in service?"

"As a firefighter. During the fire at the Bridge Farm. The whole Martin family was caught in it, even the baby who had just been born. Our Jeannot couldn't bear just standing there letting them burn, especially since he was never able to have kids with my sister. The others yelled at him that it was crazy, but he didn't want to hear it. He went into the building and he never came back out. He got a medal after he died, but a fat lot of good that did my sister."

"What caused it, the fire?"

"No one ever knew. A lamp falling over, a fire left

smoldering, who knows. Some people even say that some-one had a hand in it, since the fire started in three places and it would have been some kind of bad luck for that to happen. Who knows?"

"Did you know them, the Martins?"

"A little. The father I saw at church, but besides that he didn't go out much. The two sons a little more. The older one sold vegetables at market. We talked a lot, him and me. He always wanted to travel, Baptiste did. That would have made him happy, if he hadn't been tied to the land. He would tell us stories, that one. Stories just like in books. When there was time, we all gathered around to listen to him. Your mother too, that made her happy."

"My mother?"

"Victorine, your mother. She wouldn't miss those sto-ries for anything in the world. Poor thing. She couldn't have enjoyed herself much at your house. You could see her getting worn down, like old soap. All the same, she'd been a beauty, your mother. The rose of the village. Ev-eryone turned to look when she went by. Even me, I was happy to stop and chat with her. Then, when she chose your father. . . . I won't say he was a bad guy. But tough, that's for sure, sullen, tight-lipped, and you didn't have to be a curé to see that it wasn't going to work out for the two of them. After a few years, she never smiled anymore and she started running off with her children in tow and your father, he'd search the whole village to bring her back, his Victorine, and you could see that the two of them, together, they were driving each other crazy. It was such a pity to watch sometimes. I remember once when your sister, Maryse, who looked just like Victorine, like two drops of water, was sitting there, right across the way, you know, beside the fountain, watching them bawling at each other, and night fell and it was getting cold, and I was eating at my sister's, and I saw her through the window, and I wanted to get up and go wrap a sweater around her shoulders because it was really getting cold and dark. And finally I couldn't stand it anymore, I went out and took her some of the chicken and rice that my sister had made."

The suit fit me like a glove, the pants as well. There were shoes and a shirt that needed ironing. Looking in the mirror, I didn't recognize myself anymore. Marcel was still talking. He talked about his childhood, the village, and the present that wasn't like the past anymore, and me, I saw Victorine, my mother, who was like Maryse, that's what Marcel had said, and for the first time I had before my eyes an image that I hadn't invented or stolen or chosen at random, I had the mother I must have had in my head, and that, you've got to say, is no small thing.

→>−◂−

The bells began to ring, and there we were right in front of the church, us and Fanny's family, Fanny, that's what she was called, the wife. Since there was no mother or sister, no one took my brother's arm and linked it to the arm of his fiancée, so, just like that, in we all went along the wide path. Arthur was very pale, and his Fanny not much better, in her dress that was a bit too big, which made me realize that it wasn't the first time it had been worn, this dress, that it had belonged to someone who had entered with more courage than these two who were about to walk into the empty church. The bells were pealing and when our Roger came out to welcome us, it did me good to see someone smiling on account of the long faces that everyone was wearing here, and me not daring to let my teeth show, for fear of getting a thrashing.

She wasn't ugly or pretty, Fanny. Small, thin, so thin, almost a little kid still, with eyes all mixed green and brown so you couldn't tell what color they were. She had big hands that made you think she could work hard, and not only in the house, and wide hips, and, like they say, that's good at least for the babies so they don't get stuck inside and cause a whole lot of complications for us. Her mouth was drawn down into *a pout*, that's what that expression was called in *The Guardian Angel*.

They didn't look at each other much, my brother and his fiancée, and when their eyes met, you could see them dart the other way like scorched moths. Nevertheless, he had made himself decent, Arthur. At the last minute, he'd given up on being a slob and he'd borrowed one of the father's cardigans, which made him look like he was getting ready for a funeral, as grim as a lawyer's umbrella. Fanny's brothers stood shoulder to shoulder, as though glued to one another, and their eyes never left us, just in case anyone decided to do something stupid or to take off before the Mass was said. But it was said and said well, the Mass, and I could see that my Roger had put his whole heart into it for the lovebirds who didn't look in the least like lovebirds but really like those sentenced to life on this earth, which is more like what we are. And I loved him for that, my Roger, and for the way he had become, like someone who knows life can come crashing down on you at any moment and you can consider yourself happy if, for the moment, nothing much is going wrong.

We returned home with the girl. In the end no one wanted to celebrate, so it had all been for nothing, my cleaning the rooms one by one and beating the armchairs, which no one would ever come to sit in at our house, but me, I still felt like I was celebrating the whole way home in my good clothes, proud of the François I'd become, even if the church had been empty because this marriage, everyone knew it had already started off wrong. No one spoke on the way back, and I could see that Fanny was breathing hard in her dress and her shoes must have been hurting her, so I said, "You can take them off if you want, no one comes this way," but she shrugged her shoulders and went on as if I were nothing more than the wind.

I went back up into my room, I took off my clothes one by one, smoothing them to keep them neat and flat, like someone who pays attention, and I put my every-day clothes back on to do what I had to do, looking at the clock, because that evening, I would make a dash for Amélie's and I would finish up with the alphabet. It was good that they were all off getting lost in their own affairs and no one noticed anyone else, so I could eye the other side of the river where the Martins and their house had been and Jeannot who was dead for nothing because no one inside had been saved.

➤──◄

It was almost Christmas, and I had all the letters. I knew the *wagon* heading toward the plains, the *xylophone* that sings in your ear, and also the *Zouave* marching off to war and wondering if he will return someday. I had opened Maryse's big book, and on the first page you could see written, "To Maryse, my little cook, Maman," and that gave me a strange feeling suddenly, but it made me happy to think she had known all the words and the signs just like I did, the mother I must have had. There were stains and faint scents inside the book, and I felt that it had had a life in my sister's hands. It was all the way at the end of the book, the recipe for stuffed turkey, in "Holiday Meals." You needed a big platter, to heat the oven, a turkey, foie gras, morels, sweet wine, and shallots. I would have to go to the last village on the main road for sure, because it was bigger than ours and this wasn't the season for morels. But now, as I drove the roads, you can be sure I wasn't a bit afraid anymore.

Before leaving, I saw her through the window, Fanny, who was spending more and more of her time outdoors. No one had come to visit her since the ceremony, not her brothers or her father. In the evenings she didn't speak to anyone and she hardly ate. My brothers didn't even look at her, or the father, that goes without saying. It was as if she were an enemy, as if she should pay for all the wrongs of the women in our house, who left too soon. I wanted to say something to her or ask her how it was going, even though I knew the answer, but it was hard, getting through that shell of silence. So I watched her, I looked at her without saying anything, the wife of my brother, and in my stomach rose a great wave of pity.

→>—<←

I'd taken a sprig of holly and some tools and I'd headed down the last road, my heart pounding in my chest, and when I pushed open the gate and when I saw them all lined up in rows like they were waiting for me, that did something in my chest as well. I read what was written on the tombs, sometimes I saw photos, and that did something to me, oh yes it did, and when I read "Martin" and I saw the cross for the little one who was dead at three days old, Cyril Martin, buried the same morning as his parents, Benoît and Camille Martin, I thought, that's one sad story, that one, and when I got to the wall covered with ivy, I read "Jean-Paul Sorrente" and I knew that I'd arrived. There were weeds growing all around the iron cross, but this was it, this was where he slept, my brother, and before looking for the mother I must have had—because you shouldn't go too quickly, because if you dash headlong like a madman, your heart jumps about in your chest; each thing matters, it has to happen bit by bit like the planted wheat that gradually breaks through the soil, or else you vomit and what happens to you doesn't do you any good—I chose to clean up the place. Scraping back the soil that was there where you wouldn't expect it, pulling the weeds that had no business here, cutting what was overgrown. It took me quite some time, that work, and I made myself keep my eyes shut tight or glued to my little patch of ground, so that I could open them wide when I had finished and finally turn my gaze to the mother I must have had. When that was all done, the tomb was as beautiful as a bed all made and waiting for you. I ventured a glance to the right, and it was marked "Ghislaine Dusecours"; that wasn't my mother's name, for sure. On the other side, it was "Jérôme Manfrou," the priest before Roger, and no need even to wonder there. I picked up my shovel and rake and walked up and down the little paths to find her, my Victorine, but it was like a game of hide-and-seek where it's already been decided you'll lose, because there were no more Victorines there than there are whales in a henhouse. I didn't understand it. I didn't understand it at all, and I stood frozen to the gravel path. Maybe my mother had been buried outside the village then, or not buried at all, which seemed to me worse, because when you're not buried, they say, your soul wanders through the countryside, through the grass that thrashes in the wind. No one knows where to mourn for you, and you, you can never rest. With that, my shoulders sagged without me even thinking about it, and my legs felt sad and heavy, but they wanted to know the truth, my legs, they were determined to clear this up, so they carried me straight to Roger's house, where he was in his courtyard splitting wood, and like that, with his sleeves rolled up, you could see the veins sticking out in his arms. From time to time he pushed his hair back with his wrist and if you hadn't seen the cross at his neck, you'd never imagine what he did in his life, Roger.

→>-<+

I was standing behind him and when I called his name, he jumped like the devil, I frightened him so, and I remembered the day old Mahieu died, when Roger was wriggling about in the bushes, struggling like a sissy, and it showed in moments like that how he'd come from the city and he'd never completely get used to it here. Afterwards he gave me a smile as if to apologize and he invited me inside for a beer, between us men. For a long time no one said anything, and I think that Roger was looking at me, and after more and more minutes passed, he asked me in a very gentle voice, "How are you, François? It's no picnic, this business." And for a few seconds I didn't understand what he meant, and then the pieces fell into place and I answered, "That's how it goes," on account of Fanny and my brother, because there was nothing to be done and even less to say. But Roger, he wanted to talk and to say a whole load of things, and he talked and talked, and I could see that it didn't really interest him, my brother and his Fanny, it was really the woman, the woman in the night, the woman that he had lost, and the baby with her, and that sometimes you don't know what to do, you want something and everything goes wrong just when everything seemed possible. And I couldn't say anything to him since I knew all about it, so all I could do was keep my mouth shut and play dumb like I didn't understand. But then I spoke up.

"I was at the cemetery looking for my mother, and nothing."

He looked surprised. "What, your mother?"

"I want to know where she's buried, if she isn't here."

"Your mother?"

"My mother, Victorine Sorrente."

"That was before I got here. I'll go look, there are reg-isters, maybe it's marked. When did she die, your mother?"

"I don't know. After I was born, since I'm here. But not long after, since I don't remember anything about her."

"And when were you born, François?"

"Seventeen years ago, Roger, when the night is the shortest."

"In June?"

"In June, that's it."

He went to find the old books filled with tricky hand-writing that ran across all the pages, and he flipped back to the year of my birth and turned the pages. When he came to the day I was born and dipped into the water, he read me the whole thing, that Sorrente François Marie was born at Saint-Paul-des-Eaux on the twenty-first of June, son of Jacques Marie Sorrente, farmer, and Victorine Ghislaine Dufour, no profession. On the same page there was also Martin Cyril Marie, and I thought that it could just as well have been me who had roasted like a pig on a spit in the fire at the Bridge Farm. We turned page after page after page, and nothing, nothing at all, not a trace of Victorine Sorrente. We looked back further, much further, in another old book, and Roger and me, we saw clearly that she had existed, my mother, since she was born on December 16, Dufour Victorine Ghislaine, daughter of Louis Marie Dufour, postman, and Bernadette Marie, foundling. And that did something to me when Roger read it because I began to imagine them in my head, the postman and the foundling.

"I don't see anything anywhere," said Roger. "It's a real mystery."

"Could it be possible that she isn't dead, Roger?"

"Yes, it's possible. Anything is possible, if anyone knows that, it's me."

"How do I find out the truth, Roger?"

"Hmm . . . I imagine your father or your brothers must know something."

"I don't know."

"What do you mean, you don't know?"

"The only time I asked where my mother was, the father gave me such a telling off that I never wanted to ask again."

"You're a man now, François. It's time to stop being afraid of your father. You've made friends with words now."

"I don't dare."

"What do you mean you don't dare, François?"

"It's true, Curé, it scares the pants off me. The father, he'll go livid, that's for sure."

"I'll go for you, if you want."

"You're crazy, Roger."

"He doesn't scare me, your father."

"It's not a good idea, Roger. With Maryse, when you came, everything went wrong."

"That was different. Don't worry, François. Tomorrow I'll go talk to him."

I wanted to ask him right then and there how it was different, but something in my head told me to hush up because it isn't good to fill in all the gaps at once. So I went back home with all these open questions.

⇥⥽⥼⇤

I was there at market in the last village on the main road and I had seen a booth where they sold morels preserved in oil, and that made me think that they were exactly what would bring me happiness, and my family happiness, and maybe even Fanny whose hands were red from the cold. I'd done a good business that morning, even though it was the first time I'd set up my booth there, because in our village, people told stories about this village and its inhabitants, they didn't like them very much. Not at all, in fact, if you get my meaning. It went back to the war, what they said. A schoolteacher had hidden an aviator there, or something like that, but the mayor of the village had supposedly reported them to the enemy who, they said, came into the school and opened fire. All the children were killed, the aviator and the schoolteacher as well, and the inhabitants of the village still lived under that curse, according to the stories. Or sometimes it was a case of the water being poisoned by the curé because every twenty generations there was at least one curé who went completely bonkers, that was for sure, or maybe it was simply that the villagers there were richer than we were, seeing as they sold morels, they had factories, and the village looked more like a town, so when we went there, we felt lost. . . . Who knows.

But my cheeses sold well there, and I told myself I would close up fifteen minutes early to get the morels, and just as I thought that, I saw her with her basket, the woman who had pushed me away in the dark, she was wearing a skirt, and over the skirt a big coat and a shawl that wrapped around her whole body, and she was tired and pale as well. She didn't see me right away, she was looking at the sheep cheeses, but I kept my eyes on her, then the moment when she looked up she turned even paler, but I gave her a smile, a nice smile that said, "You don't have to be afraid," so the color returned to her cheeks and I spoke: "Would you like something?" and since she hesitated, I held out a cheese with herbs: "Take this, it's full of vitamins," and since she didn't know if she should take it or not, I said, "It's a gift," and I put it in her bag myself. She smiled with her mouth going all wrong like when you're about to cry, because she must have remembered that it was me who helped Roger across the square, just as I suddenly understood that it was her voice I'd heard when my Roger, bare-chested, stuck his head out the window. Then I smiled again and again because there was nothing else to do, and I said, "It'll all be alright once it's over, Sybille," just like that, without thinking, and when I heard myself say it, I thought that Roger had been ever so right because now I was the friend of words, they rose up in me all by themselves, and I thought that if I had had them for Oscar, I would have whispered so many things to my pig while the light in his eyes was going out. I would have said to him, "You are my friend, Oscar, even if I'm your friend who was fooled like you were by my brother, because we were both fooled, you and me, because we were taken by the feet in that old story of man and beast, men who kill beasts because they don't know how to do anything else, but you must not be afraid, my Oscar, it's not for nothing, this pain, my pig, because I see it, I do, I keep it in my head, I keep you in my head and in my heart as well, which is pounding right now, because for me, you are not a beast, Oscar, a bag of skin and bone about to become ham, no, you will always be my Oscar, and if I could, I would go with you, here and now, I would accompany you, because it's not worth a thing, this life, when you can't defend your friend." When I stopped thinking all this, the woman was still there in front of me, and she must have said something to me or asked me a question because she looked like she was waiting for me to open my mouth, then she repeated, "Do you come every week?" and I don't know why but I said yes, so then it was decided, I was going to come back here, without fail, to this last village on the main road. Then after dismantling my stall, I went and bought them, the morels.

Driving home, I saw him from a distance walking at a snail's pace, so oddly, as if he had emptied the barrel at the Café de la Place, which didn't surprise me and made me feel sorry for him, thinking to myself, he doesn't even care how he looks anymore, poor Roger, and his cassock was in a state, the collar half off, his hair a mess, not a shred of respectability—really, Roger, what the heck?—and then, looking at his face, I saw the bloody cut above his eye and his flattened nose, his face was purple, my Roger, and no, this wasn't wine or beer but wretched fists, maybe even a stick or pitchfork, and I didn't have to think very hard to guess what had happened to him.

"He really got me . . ."

"What the heck . . . ?"

"'If you think you're going to scare me by stirring up old stories,' that's what your father said. I didn't come to stir up anything at all, only to find out where she is, Victorine. 'There's nothing to find out, Curé. But if you think you can threaten me, you're wrong, and you can say what you want, Roger, about Victorine disappearing and the fire and all that, no one will believe you, no one saw anything, you hear me? And then there's prescription, you know what prescription is, Curé? So don't you dare come back here, Curé, don't you dare. You better not dare come near us, the Sorrentes, don't even think about it. Or else I'll tell my sons to do you in. Don't think you're any smarter than the last curé. It's bad luck to go sticking your nose in other people's business. You understand that, Curé?'"

"And what did you say then, Roger?"

"That I did understand, François. That I understood very well, and I took off without waiting to hear more. I was wrong, François. It doesn't do any good to talk to him.

No good at all. They're nuts at your place. If I hadn't run, they really might have broken my legs."

There was no more to say, so Roger climbed into the van and I took him back to his house. And it seemed like we'd done this before, him and me, on account of the times I'd driven him home when he was completely smashed and he couldn't remember a thing anymore.

→►◄←

They were all there around the supper table and the words, "That wasn't right to do that to Roger," remained stuck in my throat, but I would have said them if it would have served some purpose, besides getting my face bashed in too. So I just muttered, "I brought morels," and since Christmas was three days away, I laid out my idea for them of the stuffed turkey, and I saw right away that something lit up in Fanny's eyes, and in Arthur's as well, since he loved to devour whatever fell into his hands.

That evening we stayed after to clean up, Fanny and me, even though it wasn't my job anymore since she was there, but even so, as words were rising up in me all on their own, it would be good to have someone to hear them, and I could see by her look that here was someone to listen. At first, she scrubbed the dishes, looking down at the washtub, and I dried them in silence, seeing as it was up to her to say something since the last time it had been me, when I had whispered to her that she could take them off, the shoes with the flowers on them that hurt her feet, so much so that they turned red, her feet, and surely they weren't hers, those shoes, but someone else's, from another wedding, where people laughed and danced away their cares. Just because someone has the shoes of happiness doesn't mean that happiness comes with them, that's what I was thinking as I dried my cup, and I saw something rise in Fanny's throat, a sigh, and I could see clearly that her heart was full, but that didn't make me decide to speak, because I knew Fanny, she could suddenly shrug her shoulders and make like I didn't exist, and at times like those, you feel like you're a total idiot, like all your gentleness was being trampled in the mud. So I would rather keep quiet. There were cups to dry and the only sound you could hear was the water rinsing the plates, knives, forks, spoons, and pots in the sink. She stood there looking at the dishes, and I wiped the plates and the pots with my dish towel, then carried a stack of them to the sideboard and took my place again beside Fanny. Ever since words had started coming to me, silence didn't frighten me anymore, maybe because I knew that I could chase it away with almost nothing, whereas before, it had clung tight to my very bones. With Fanny, it was a gentle silence, although I could see well enough that she wasn't happy here, like all of us for whom happiness had fled. When we were all finished, and the water had drained from the tub, and everything was tidy, Fanny put out the light and we went up to bed without a word.

The next day, I was there beside her once again, by the washtub, and I had decided that I would dry dishes until she finally spoke to me. Why, I didn't know. But she would speak to me, and I would say things that no one had heard me say before. I had gotten it into my head, that thought, so that it would never be in vain to wash the glasses, pottery, pewter, copper, and iron pots, everything that was useful to us without being beautiful. But it wasn't going to be that evening that anyone would speak. I could see that well enough by how her eyes kept looking toward the floor and everything that's in the earth. No, it wasn't going to be that evening, and I thought that Christmas was coming and it was getting colder and colder and maybe it would snow tomorrow, that all the animals were in, and that we had to roll towels in front of the doors to keep the wind from settling into our bones. When we were all done, I helped Fanny drain the tub, I put away the brush, straightened the floorcloth, and just as I was putting out the light to go upstairs, I heard her voice, all thin, like a sob, whispering, "Thank you, François." It was dark, so I couldn't see her features very well, but I saw her, Fanny, small and slender in the big stairway, so I answered, "Sure thing, Fanny, good night."

The next day I had market, where I would set up my stand across from Marcel's and, day by day, I was getting to like these times on the squares when I got to see those faces again that were becoming familiar to me, to hear stories that got told from village to village, where I caught the odors of chickens roasting, flowers, spices that you don't smell anywhere else. Marcel's face was all red that morning, you could tell without him even turning around that his fever had gotten into his very bones, shivering as he was in his gray pullover, so I settled him in my van and I ran between the two stalls all morning long, my sack full of change bulging at my waist so that no one could take it, or else I'd have a sorry Christmas in store for me. That was quite a chore and it kept me warm all morning, and that was something at least, for the moment. I saw her coming toward me and I noticed right away that she'd dressed up, Amélie, she was wearing a hat with a red flower and a red shawl and red shoes. She looked like a mill, dressed like that, and I didn't know if I liked her better as a mill or on normal days, when you could see she was a little faded and bulging like a cask, but suddenly there she was in front of me, and she was smiling at me, and I thought to myself that a smile is a gift you have to take, no questions asked, or else you won't get by. "Merry Christmas, François," and she took a wrapped present from her coat and gave it to me. That made me feel strange, especially since what with the turkey, the morels, Roger, all that, I had almost forgotten Amélie, so I grabbed a bunch of mistletoe that Marcel had hung over his stall and I said, "Happy holidays, Amélie, happy holidays," and I held it out to her. Then she took it, held it over her head, and said, "Do you want to kiss me, François?" I turned as red as the holly berries beside me, but I kissed her even so, under the mistletoe, because you can't do anything else, it brings good luck, and you can never have too much of that. I was afraid that someone might be watching us or would whistle at us, but apparently no one was interested because I didn't hear a thing. After the kiss, Amélie was still clinging to me for what seemed too long, as if she were going to swallow me, so I pushed her away a little and said, "Thanks for the present, Amélie, but I have to work." She answered, "That's OK, François," bought some eggs and cheese from me, and left. At the end of the morning, I'd done a crazy business because it was

Christmas and people are always afraid of the winter cold and can't help stocking up. I woke Marcel in my van, he was feeling a little better. I turned down the money he wanted to give me because I was so proud of having run two stalls by myself, me, who used to be an airhead with only pigs for friends.

On the way home, I saw smoke rising from old Lucie's house, and I thought to myself that it must have been a long time since she had shared a Christmas dinner with anyone. I wasn't going to invite her to our house, because everyone would have scowled, except maybe Fanny, and that wasn't even for sure. I could at least bring her a sausage and some parsley or at least take her arm to help her in from the garden. I stopped the van, knocked on the door, heard "Come in," and stuck my head inside. It was completely dark in there, I didn't know where to step, I went straight ahead, then I felt myself knocking into something, so I cried, "Ouch!" and recognized an old laugh, like a little bell, and her voice: "Is that you, François?"

"You can't see a thing in here," I said, rubbing my leg.

"You're in my darkness, François."

"It doesn't make you afraid, Lucie?"

"You get used to it, François. You can get used to anything. How are things at your house?"

"OK, Lucie, OK."

"And the little one? She's holding up?"

"Not so well, Lucie, not so well."

I heard a big sigh that meant, "That will pass," because everything always ends up passing in any case, even grief, even joy.

"What did you bring, François?"

It seemed strange to me that she said that, old Lucie who ordinarily always knew what I was bringing, and I thought to myself that old age takes us all, each in our turn, and that the day comes when old witches must die as well.

"It's Christmas soon," I said.

Then I heard her get up, her old bones creaking and the ringing of her heavy shoes on the floor coming in my direction. I guessed she was feeling her way toward me, so I held out my parsley and sausage for her, she took them with one hand and then placed the other hand on my shoulder and for a moment she said nothing, and then I felt her rough mouth against my mouth, that did something in the pit of my stomach, and I thought that this was the second time today I received a kiss. I also thought to myself that I was beginning to get used to her odor of moss, old Lucie's, because moss is like a carpet you can lie down on and it will never hurt you, right? I also thought that I didn't know what to do next, if I ought to leave, to say something, stay there, or what, but it was old Lucie who opened her mouth first, so then there was nothing to worry about anymore.

"You're like your father, you are, François. The kindness of your father, the care of your father. I loved him right away, your father, open, willing to help, not an ounce of pretension. I loved Benoît right off."

"Jacques," I said, "my father is Jacques. You're getting old, Lucie."

"That's not who I'm talking about."

"Who then?"

"Benoît of the Bridge Farm, Benoît from the other side of the river, Benoît, his hair in the wind when I could still see, and who sang along the paths when he was coming back from Camille's. They had known each other from childhood, those two, were meant for each other, people said. So no one was surprised when they announced their wedding. It was summer, a celebration, a celebration, François, like we never have in the village anymore. And then they waited for you, waited a long time. They almost gave up, but one day you were on your way. She had become light-hearted again, Camille, and then, you see how luck turns, how luck turns . . ."

In my head too, it began to turn, turn flat-out nuts, if

you see what I mean, and although it was totally dark, I felt a huge light in my head and then something like a shock and something that gave way under me, the floor or simply my knees. She kept talking to me, talking to me, old Lucie, and her voice was like the river in my head roiling fast as it flowed, and you try to drown it out and you can't do it.

→>—<←

I woke up in my own bed, and when I saw Fanny's face bent over my forehead with a moist cloth, at first I cried out and then no, it's Fanny, it's only Fanny, I said to myself, then I gave her a smile and she smiled back, and all of a sudden she added, "Merry Christmas, François," and I understood that it was all over for the stuffed turkey. She asked if I wanted anything, some water, some soup or bread, but none of that mattered to me, I looked at Fanny and I wondered who I was now, it might be that Lucie had told me a pack of lies, but maybe not, what good would that do her now, I ask you, and then, what about me, I really loved her, Lucie who had come to our house after I was born. If old Lucie spoke the truth, and every part of me wanted to believe it, my feet, my hands, my back, my legs, and all the little things it takes ages to name, then I was the son of Benoît and Camille of the Bridge Farm, I wasn't the son of Victorine-the-unhappy-one who wandered about the countryside and Jacques with the knife-sharp face, I wasn't the brother of Jean-Paul who threw himself off the roof because Arthur had told the father that he had caught him in the pig barn and then called him nothing but queer, fag, whore, even though Maryse covered my ears so that I wouldn't hear, but what were my ears for, I wasn't the brother of Arthur who hitched up girls' skirts and even less the brother of Jules who had killed my Oscar. I wasn't the child that didn't look like anyone and that everybody forgot in the photos. I was the son of Benoît who sang along the paths, his hands in his pockets, his hair blowing in the wind, who wasn't afraid of the flowing water. I was the son of Camille who had loved me as a wonder, happy to have me in her belly and feel me wriggling like a little devil. I was the son of the Martins from the other side of the water, and it could be that I had their eyes, their hands, their teeth, and their smile. The only thing that twisted my insides into knots was that Maryse would no longer be anything to me, and that, that wasn't possible, any more than forgetting her hand through my hair, or when she said "Fifi," or when she tied my shoelaces so gently or gave me the lunch she'd packed for the day and inside there was always some treat to nibble on. It was like a cloth full of holes in my head, there were some answers to my questions, but also darkness and complete mysteries, more mysterious than before when I had accepted life as it was without asking questions. Now there was nothing but questions, like a big game where you know in advance that you're going to lose, like, if I'm Cyril Martin, then where is François Sorrente? And what about that fire? And who set it? And Jacques and Victorine, what did they have to do with all that? As I closed my eyes, Fanny, she got worried, she said, "Are you OK, François?" so I nodded yes because it would take too long to explain. And suddenly I remembered the present from Amélie that I'd left in the van and suddenly I wanted to see it, that present, because it was Christmas after all, even for me who had been lost in the fog and who had woken up exactly the same even though I was someone else. I didn't know if the van was parked by our house since last I knew it had been waiting in front of old Lucie's place, but apparently it was, because Fanny returned with the red package. In my hands it felt heavier than at market when she'd given it to me, Amélie, but maybe it was because I was lighter right now, floating on a cloud, removed from it all. I opened the present carefully, saving the paper with the angels on it, which could be used again. It was like gray down, knitted, a scarf to go around your neck, and you could see at first glance that the hands with the rings had knitted it themselves, and there were strands of soft, sparkling angel hair yarn, and suddenly I thought that life was beautiful. Not beautiful like something you look at in a shop window that doesn't belong to you, that will never belong to you and that scoffs at you and says, "Not for you, kid"; beautiful like something bloody that takes you by chance, that flays you, but that's how life is when you're at the heart of it, when something happens and it happens to you, then you can say that life is beautiful.

I raised my head and looked at Fanny, I said to her, "Merry Christmas. Merry Christmas, Fanny," and her mouth began to tremble and break into a thousand pieces. There was a flood of tears and words, all the words she'd been holding in that I knew she would finally let out someday. All that she had wanted was to leave, to get away from them all, because that's no life, slaving away like that, slaving worse than the beasts, because that's a stupid life, so she'd said anything to get Arthur, anything at all, because he had liked her, used to like her, really hadn't liked her at all actually, but now what was done was done, she had gotten herself into the very same mess and there was no going back now, she wanted to throw herself in the river or worse or anything at all, it didn't matter. . . . Then she was crying and crying again and then she said, "Save me, François, save me," and if one thing was impossible, that was it. That I could save her, because I couldn't save anyone, not Oscar or Jean-Paul or all the others you love, that you can't keep from dying like flies that get flattened with a slap. I didn't even know if you could save yourself, but I was willing to believe you could. I wanted to believe that. Already I knew how to read and I no longer hung my head. There really was a meadow on this earth where I could be happy without owing anyone anything. So I took her in my arms, Fanny, I hugged her gently, I wiped the tears from her eyes, I stroked her hair and then her whole body because there's nothing else you can do so long as you're alive, and it was Christmas after all.

→>–<+

I could not fix Fanny's life, but I could take her to old Lucie's, where no one would dare to go look for her. She would be better off there than at our house. Early the next morning, I left her there just like that, before the wooden door, shivering, frail, and blond in the red dawn. If I must hold on to an image of Fanny, that will be the one.

Afterwards, I raced right to my Roger's house. I knocked and knocked, there was no one home. All the same, this was the day after Christmas, and it was only eight o'clock. I was worried that my Roger might have gone off his rocker again, abusing his body for nothing, so I went in through the back door, which was always open, as he'd said to me one day, just in case, "The back door is always open, François." It was, in fact, open, wide open, the back door, as though to invite thieves, but taking a look around, that was no surprise since there was nothing at all left in there, as if someone had just cleared out. Though the big furniture, the curé's tables and chests that had known the last curé who had taken a beating, and the one before him and the one before him, sat there tall and dark in their old brown way, all the small things that told of Roger's life, they had all disappeared: glasses, books, clothes, brush, soap, quilt. . . . Everything that made this house belong to my friend. The bike as well, it wasn't there anymore. . . . It looked like someone had just taken off, and it must have just happened since our Roger must have said the midnight Mass, or else our village would have been turned upside down, gossiping and searching for him on all our four roads.

There were a thousand things to imagine, that our Roger had cleared out for fear of scandal and that, after tossing his cassock in the nettles, he had slunk off like a rat keeping low to the ground as he crossed the fields, or that maybe he had gone and hung himself along some narrow path where no one would find him until spring, gray, bloated, eyes gouged out by the sparrows, but that was a horrible thing to imagine about someone who was my friend, that's what I said to myself as I headed toward the door, because there was nothing else for me to do but to leave his place and go break a church window to get to them, the big leather books, and to find out for myself what I suspected, and heading toward the door, on the big chest right beside it, I saw it, left there for me, just like that, and I knew that he hadn't gone off for nothing, my Roger, because you don't go off to hell and leave your friend *The Inn of the Guardian Angel* by the Countess Rostopchine, who tells you that there's always a crust of bread waiting for you somewhere when it's cold, arms to hold you, fresh linens, and children to tuck in even if you no longer have a family.

I preferred to think that my Roger had left for another life, with his Sybille, the woman with the gentle voice who whispered, "My love, my love," in the dark, because you can never leave a voice like that without hearing it and following it, because everyone has a right to love, even me, even Fanny, even Hyménée, even old Lucie, if that's possible, and a woman's child deserves to have a father, a father who loves him, like I had been loved by Benoît and Camille, my parents who loved each other and didn't run about the countryside in all directions looking for who knows what or stories that would make you forget your cares. I preferred to think that my Roger had rented a van like mine, that he had loaded all his things while we slept and then he had opened the van door so the woman could climb in, in a beautiful white dress with a light scarf, polka-dotted, and that they were headed south, where it was sunny, where you see grass growing greener than here, where no one yells at you if you ask questions, where no one would ever know he was a poor devil in a cassock, my Roger, who experienced grief just like anyone else because sometimes his god abandoned him.

That's what I was thinking as I threw the rock to break the stained glass window that would lead me right to the sacristy, where I would find it, the confounded book that would let me unravel the last knots in my history. I had to break two of them, my aim was so bad on account of all my feelings, and my fear and anger after all that time wasted, and finally when the noise of the breaking glass died down, I climbed along the wall, then leaned into the gaping hole and landed in the middle of the broken shards. I crossed to the altar covered with flowers and Christmas banners, glanced at the baby Jesus sleeping in complete faith in the manger, even though faith, you know it'll poke you in the eye just when you're not looking, and I felt sorry for him, naked in the cold with the broken windows, but it was too late for that now. I entered the sacristy and I saw them all lined up, the magnificent leather tomes. I had to find mine, the one with my birth, to be sure of what I had felt deep within ever since old Lucie had spoken those words to me.

There were plenty of them, those books, heavy and dusty and filled with the names of hundreds of Martins and Sorrentes, going back years and years, since before the Flood. I didn't find the right one immediately, and my impatience made me take down the ones on either side although afterwards I realized that the one I wanted had been right in front of me all along. That's how life is, I thought, the secret of secrets is always right in front of you, and it's as if your eyes are misted over or filled with smoke or soot, and you spend your time groping about like a simpleton who understands nothing.

And I came to the page for June 21. And on the page for June 21, there were two names of children: Cyril Martin and François Sorrente, because the day on which Cyril Martin was declared dead at three days of age, although no one had found the body, François Sorrente, age of three days, was declared born. Now, for the babies in our village, children born at the Sorrentes' or children born at the Martins', they were declared on the day of their birth, that was always the case since they were also baptized at home, so that they couldn't be stricken by life and death in the same cold blow and find themselves in hell by the worst of all fates. Cyril Martin had been declared June 18 at the Bridge Farm, by his father Benoît and his mother Camille. But the child François Sorrente had been brought to the presbytery by his sister, Maryse Sorrente, at three days old, and when I read that in the big leather book my heart began to founder because it realized what it may have always known, that there had only ever been one baby, the one who had been born at the Martins' and who had been raised by the Sorrentes, the one whose picture was never taken with Victorine Sorrente, dead in the fire at the Bridge Farm, one night when she was sleeping beside Baptiste Martin, who told her stories of travels at the markets where she ran, breathless and hopelessly in love, to escape Jacques Sorrente, who had made her life a misery. Even so the baby had been saved from the flames, and maybe the blond woman of the farm, she hadn't been there for nothing, and Marcel's brother-in-law, Jeannot, maybe he hadn't gone up in smoke for nothing either, that's what I told myself, feeling the tears running down my face, while the large letters in the book began dancing before my eyes, dancing the jig, because life, I said to myself, life is always escaping you, you think you know it and you don't know it at all.

I thought too that it was Maryse, my own Maryse, even though she was no longer mine through blood since I had become the child of the Martins, Maryse who had held me in her arms, who had carried me all by herself to the curé, the curé who would catch hell for it a few days later, and I didn't have to think very hard to imagine who had taken a spade to his head in the curve of a narrow path. And I thought again that surely it was Maryse who had followed the father when she heard the door slam one night and who had walked behind him in her thin nightshirt, had crossed the bridge and had slid down into the high grass while he started the fire at the Bridge Farm, furious as he was, completely crazy because of his Victorine who no longer loved him, him and his four children, who maybe had never loved him but had only wanted to escape a miserable childhood and had gotten herself back into the same mess like girls often do when they dream about love stories and princesses, maybe like Maryse who had learned to read and who knew them, those stories, that my Roger had given her, and for her it was *After the Rain, Blue Skies* by that same Countess of Ségur who had taught me that there was always a place for lost children. Maryse had told it to me, that story of a young girl who had suffered all her life, and that was the rain, and then one day the sun appeared from behind the clouds and all her troubles vanished. "There are those, Fifi, who are happy at first and then it's a trail of misfortunes. It won't be that way for us, Fifi. We will be happy." Maryse had heard the wooden beams cracking and the wind stoking the flames, licking the trees and the whole surrounding countryside. She must have heard the cries, oh yes, the terrible cries of those who are dying; I know them too, I know those cries. She, Maryse, who must have called old Lucie right afterwards, because how do you take care of a child, she didn't know, Maryse, but Lucie showed her and taught her. Maryse who had wanted to look after me and had had the idea of baptizing me François Sorrente since I had no one left anymore. And the father must have agreed that I could grow up there, agreed and said nothing, agreed so that no one would talk anymore. Jean-Paul had kept his mouth shut, as he kept his mouth shut about everything, Jules too, and Arthur was still too little. In the village no questions were asked. It was no surprise, Victorine's leaving, as unhappy as she was, always wandering the roads; or my birth either, out of nowhere, I must have arrived early, that's why no one had known anything about that pregnancy, swift as a runaway horse on the road . . .

→-≺-

At that moment, I wondered how you recognized a mother, what made her a mother. At what moment do you say: that one, she's a mother. Recognizing a pig is simple. You can see that it's a pig, even if it has lost a leg or an ear, even if it stops grunting or just lies there asleep with its mouth open. And I thought that I didn't really know what a mother was. I'd had one for sure, for three days, who had surely cried out in pain like Daisy and Dora, exhausted by labor but afterwards calmed by resting her head against mine. A loving mother who had ironed the sheets, knitted small clothes, like Amélie's scarf, soft and velvety as silk, who had sung in my ear at night, who had given me her milk like cows do, and who had then gone up in smoke. Three days in a lifetime, that's not much when you think about it. And I know people often say it's the quality that counts. It doesn't matter if you don't have as many cheeses as the farm in the next village if yours are better. Because it's better to have a few good cheeses than a lot of bad ones, because once they've tasted yours, they won't want the ones from the farmer in the other village, that's what Jules told me, that's what he drilled into my head, same for your ham and sausage because if the pig was happy, it will only make it better, that's why it had to be Oscar's turn, that was the only reason. But three days, what was that in a lifetime, considering all the years with Maryse, who had pulled me from the ashes, Maryse who was fifteen years older than me, Maryse to whom the father had said, "Your place is here, because we need a woman, we don't have one anymore, so now it's here, your place." And for all those years, she stayed there, Maryse, within the confines of the kitchen, preparing the meals, doing the laundry, taking care of the little ones and the father, because someone had to take care of him, the father, like Victorine had, only I think maybe our Maryse did it better, just seeing how angry he was and his despair when she cleared out. Because Maryse never weighed a thing, she never took up any space, she loved flowers and the sky, she smiled at the animals, she didn't like it when the father sharpened the big knife to slaughter them, one time I even found her in the kitchen, her two hands over her ears so she couldn't hear the squealing of the pig whose throat was being slit, she was like that, my Maryse. I can't forget that Maryse combed my hair in the morning, that she asked me, "Did you brush your teeth, my Fifi?" That she stroked my forehead and lit the lamp when I woke in the night, my head full of burning grass and houses collapsing with a huge crack, that she said, "I'm here, my Fifi, I'm here, soon it'll be morning, you must not be afraid." Maryse who read me stories in books, and now I wonder how she had learned to read in that family where the mother was forever wandering the roads and the father never spoke to anyone, sometimes there are miracles even if my Roger, he would say that that doesn't count, in our lives strange things occur that will always remain mysteries. Maryse who, one day, crossed the river because she couldn't stand it any longer. Maryse whom nobody talked about anymore, but whom I hadn't forgotten. Maryse who had a room waiting for her because I said to the room, "You are Maryse's room," and I also told the bed and the curtains and the window, the walls and the light and everything that had known her close up or from far away. Maryse who, one night, had saved me from the flames and who had taken me at three days old to the curé's where I'd been baptized a second time, and when you're baptized a second time, it's as though you're born again. And if you're born again, it's as though you have a new mother. My Roger had told me about those birds that chose the first one they set eyes on to be their mother, and I'm sure for me, the first one I set eyes on must have been Maryse. And now I know why the sound of Maryse's boots in the water wrenched my heart, because you can't let your mother take off like that, you can't let her go to the other side and do nothing. I had sensed that Maryse would never come back, even though I had waited for her throughout each passing day. No one had ever come down the main road.

Now I had the letters, all the letters and the words. I was no longer bonkers. I was no longer a dumb beast. I was still afraid. You're always afraid, that doesn't leave you as long as you live. But this was a different kind of fear.

→>−<+

So, I left the sacristy, I raced like a madman all the way down our road, the sun had mostly risen, but everyone was sleeping off their wine and sausage from the night before, and there was no danger of being seen, so I dashed up to my room, collected the warmest clothes I had, the market money, that would get me started, the accordion, you never knew when it might be useful, I grabbed some bread and cheese for the road, a bottle of wine, and just like that I tore down the stairs and out to the barn. It's true that I'd said if I ever left it would be with a newborn pig on my shoulders, but I was a man now. I could only go alone. I was a man, but she was my friend. And she was the only one I was going to say good-bye to. I looked at her there among her own. Like that, you would never have said that there was anything special about her, she looked so much like the others, and if you aren't careful, a pig will always be a pig, nothing to bother about too much or to nestle your head against. I drew closer and put my arms around her neck, pressed my face against hers, and said, "I can't bring you with me where I'm going. But I won't forget you. And as soon as I've found her again, Maryse, I'll write you, I'll write you a story and everyone will know that I had a friend and her name was Hyménée. Now I have to find her, the one who is my own, that's my place, just as your place is to be here, with your own. And when the big moment arrives, don't be afraid, don't be afraid." She understood. I'm sure she understood. I had a hard time pulling my face away from hers, my arms were covered with her mud, her smell, her gentleness. I was hers as she was mine. But you can't stay forever. That much I'd come to understand.

I really did have to cross it, that confounded river, I had to see the other side, even though I'd made a promise never to go there, but to whom, I ask you—did he matter, the one who had destroyed an entire family? I had to go and see the place where I was born, the place where it had all started and then beyond, where Maryse had gone, where she was living now, to find her again, to see her eyes again that I could no longer remember so well sometimes, but that laughed with the wind, blue eyes like you sometimes find along the edges of the paths. Someday, maybe sooner, maybe later when my hair would be gray and my back would be bent, I'd arrive at some village and I'd say, "I'm looking for Maryse," and they'd say, "Who?" and I'd say, "Maryse, with delicate hands and a gentle voice and eyes you could drown in, they're so blue, and a smile that makes everything alright," then they'd say, "Oh, Maryse with the long hair," and they'd point to a building and I'd know that was it, and when I reached it and pushed open the door I'd see her from behind, bent over her ironing, or braiding a loaf of bread, or maybe reading, and her back I'd recognize immediately, as one in a thousand, because your mother's back, you always recognize it, even if your mother's old or tired or sad or alone or poor or abandoned, you can't forget that back, so I'd say, very softly, "Maryse," and maybe with a start and without turning around she would say, "Oh, Fifi, it's you."

I was already at the far end of the field and already I felt it, that strong current, so strong that it swept everything along with it, and it frightened me all the same, even though I was now a man and all that water just had to rush right over my back, it was impossible for me to drown, that's what I told myself. I pulled the soft gray scarf a little closer around my neck, felt the teeth of my Oscar imprinted in my bones, and I looked back, I saw the meadow, the dead tree, and an unlit house where strangers were still sleeping on Christmas morning—I couldn't call them anything other than that, "strangers"—now I found myself right at the edge, the edge of the earth, the edge of the high grass, the riverbank was already giving way under my weight, I looked straight ahead to the old burned buildings that had witnessed my birth, the hill, and the forest, then I looked down and stepped into the river. It was cold.

ACKNOWLEDGMENTS

Thanks to Jean-Philippe Collard-Neven, Maurice Lippens, Martine Potencier, Émile Lansman, Michel Lambert, Priscilla Trupia, Sylvie Évrard, Luce Wilquin, and the whole Éditions Luce Wilquin team, as well as François Emmanuel, for their invaluable advice and support.

Cici Olsson

GENEVIÈVE DAMAS is a Belgian actress, playwright, and novelist. She has acted, directed, and written award-winning plays for both children and adults. *If You Cross the River* is her first novel and has received wide international a cclaim. It won the Prix Victor Rossel in Belgium and the Prix des Cinq Continents de la Francophonie, awarded annually for fiction that enriches cultural diversity and the French language on the five continents. Damas lives in Brussels.

Craig Line

JODY GLADDING is the author of four collections of poems: *the spiders   my arms*, *Translations from Bark Beetle*, *Rooms and Their Airs*, and *Stone Crop*. She has translated thirty books from French, including Jean Giono's *The Serpent of Stars* and Pierre Michon's *Small Lives*, which won the French-American Foundation Translation Prize. Gladding lives in Vermont.

milkweed
editions

Founded as a nonprofit organization in 1980, Milkweed Editions is an independent publisher. Our mission is to identify, nurture and publish transformative literature, and build an engaged community around it.

We are aided in this mission by generous individuals who make a gift to underwrite books on our list. Special underwriting for *If You Cross the River* was provided anonymously.

milkweed.org

Interior design & typesetting by Mary Austin Speaker

Typeset in Fournier

Fournier is a typeface created by the Monotype Corporation
in 1924, based on types cut in the mid-eighteenth century by
Pierre-Simon Fournier, a French typographer. The specific
cuts used as a reference for Fournier are referred to as
"St Augustin Ordinaire" in Fournier's
influential *Manuel Typographique*,
published in 1764 in Paris.